WILD SUMMIT

WILD SUMMIT

Matt Stuart

GUNSMOKE

First published in the US by Dodd, Mead

This hardback edition 2011
by AudioGO Ltd
by arrangement with
Golden West Literary Agency

ISBN 978 1 445 85635 3

British Library Cataloguing in Publication Data available.

Printed and bound in Great Britain by
CPI Antony Rowe, Chippenham and Eastbourne

1.

SUNDOWN WAS LESS than an hour away when Gil Yeager cleared the monotony of the far-running, scorched-brown desert and put his horse to the swift uplift of the timber-dark country ahead.

On the long drag over the desert's arid miles he had ridden in a stoic slouch calculated to ease a man through a tiresome journey across a land holding little of interest. Here, however, with the first spicy scent of sun-warmed timber in his nostrils and the flowing, smoky shadows of approaching evening beckoning from every gulch and along each curving slope, he found new vigor, and he straightened and hungrily savored the good breath of these hills.

Erect in his saddle, he showed shoulders that were gaunt, but solid, and he was markedly spare and tightbelted about the middle, like one who had traveled far and fast on scant rations. And while his glance now reflected a swift pleasure, as though finding here a return to something well longed for, there was, couched in his angular, weather-blackened features, a settled overlay of wary harshness. The tough shadow of this same bleak reticence lay in his deep set, stone-gray eyes.

His gear showed hard usage and his clothes were worn to a faded raggedness. The bundle of possessions tied behind his saddle cantle was meagerly thin. His horse, gaunt as its rider, moved at a plodding walk along a trail which looped ever higher into the timber depths.

Here presently the way led through a marshy meadow

tucked in the timber against the hill slope and here a cold trickle of spring water was trapped in a small pool. After the brutally thirsty miles of the desert, both rider and horse drank thankfully. Moving on, he came, after another short climb, to the fence.

Newly built, the three strands of barbed wire made a tautly stretched barrier. Equally new was the sign nailed to the trunk of a towering ponderosa pine tree. What it said was blunt and to the point.

THIS TRAIL IS CLOSED!
by order of
THE SUMMIT LAND & CATTLE CO.
Meade Bastian, Mgr.

Weight slumped in one stirrup, Yeager read and reread the sign. Abruptly the pressure of a swift rising anger thinned his lips.

"Brownie," he told his horse, "that's a hell of a sign. I think I'll tear it down!"

To this he got swift, startling answer.

"Not today, mister!"

Yeager twisted in his saddle, his glance quickly seeking. Yonder past the fence a man stood half concealed behind the shadowy bole of another lofty pine, a man with a rifle couched across his arm.

"So-o!" drawled Yeager thinly. "That's the way things are, eh?"

"That's exactly the way they are," came the blunt retort.

Yeager took another look at the sign. "Meade Bastian. A new one. Used to be a fellow named Rand—Brick Rand, who bossed that thieving outfit. What happened to him? Somebody kill him? If they didn't, they should have."

"You want any answers," the man with the rifle said, "go scratch for them."

Yeager eyed the speaker bleakly and his words fell almost soft.

2

"Were you on this side of the fence I'd be tempted to take that gun and feed it to you, a foot at a time."

"But I ain't, and you won't." The rifle holder gave his weapon a threatening swing. "Scatter out of here while you're able to!"

There was nothing to do but obey. Simmering, Yeager reined off through the glooming timber, paralleling the run of the fence. He had no idea how far the wire would reach, but certainly, he reasoned, no further than Mission Grade and the stage and freight road there. Which was the route he'd now have to take, since the fence denied him the short cut he'd planned on.

Considering coldly, he knew a sharp impatience with himself. For he hadn't been too smart back there at the sign, letting his roach climb the way he did, what with the fact that the other fellow held a ready weapon while he had none. It was the temper that had done it, that swift, black fury that had become so much a part of him over the past savage year, and which could trip him up if he didn't watch it. Temper, he reflected grimly, was all right providing you bossed it, for then it could put and maintain purpose in a man. But you had to boss it!

It was full dark when he reached Mission Grade and turned into it, and evening's first stars were high and glittering by the time his weary horse put the last of the grade's dusty climb behind stumbling hoofs and across the far distance of the flat the lights of Tuscarora beckoned.

Coming in on the town there was little to make of it beyond the yellow square of a window or the rectangle of an open door shining against the black bulk of a building, yet the sight sent a gust of eagerness through Yeager. For here was home range and he'd been long away and the returning was good—good!

He rode in with caution, circling until the rancid ammoniac odors of Johnny Hock's freight and stage stables and corrals lifted strong to his nostrils. Here he unsaddled, turned his horse into a feed corral and racked his scanty gear on the fence. After which, limping with saddle stiffness, he tramped over to Johnny Hock's office.

At a lighted window he paused and peered in, to see Johnny Hock's broad back and round, bristle-haired head bent over a paper-littered desk. Yeager smiled grimly and moved on to the door of the place. Good old Johnny Hock! Ever a friend in need.

Hearing his office door open, Johnny Hock made grumbling comment without turning or looking up.

"All right—all right! I'm busy as hell—but what do you want?"

"Grub first, Johnny. After that the loan of a gun."

Grunting as though he'd been hit in his fat middle, Johnny Hock straightened and came around, all in one move. For a moment, held by surprise, he merely stared. Then he bounced to his feet.

"Gil! By all that's holy—Gil Yeager!"

He crossed the room with a rush and yanked down the window shade. Next he was at the door, pushing Yeager aside so that he might turn the key. After which he wrung Yeager's hand again and again, all the time gruffly scolding.

"Man, what are you doing here? You asking to be locked up again? Don't you know Kline Hyatt's got a five hundred dollar reward dodger out for you?"

Showing a hard grin, Yeager waited for Johnny to sputter to a stop.

"Yeah, I know about the dodger, Johnny. I've been tearing the damn thing down all the way from Two Rivers to here."

"Nothing funny about it that I can see," growled Johnny Hock severely. "I'm happy to see you, of course. But I'm scared, too. What's your idea, showing here big as life?"

"I wrote you, didn't I, that I'd be back when I got what I was after. You get my letter?"

"I got it. But I just couldn't figure you ever catching up with Shad Emmet. You did, though?"

"I did."

"And he talked?"

4

Yeager nodded. "Enough. Now, how about that grub—and a gun?"

"The grub makes sense," Johnny Hock said. "But I don't like the idea of the gun. That sort of thing can earn you more trouble."

Yeager moved restlessly to the center of the room, raw hunger a deep, almost feverish shine in his eyes.

"You let me worry about that, John. Though it can wait. Right now it's food I need. Last time I ate was yesterday noon. I ran across a sheep camp out in the desert and the Basque staked me to a plate of mutton and beans. Even before that I hadn't been what you'd call eating hearty. Yeah, I could really stand a meal."

Johnny Hock went to the door. "Lock this after me. Else somebody might blunder in, then go shout the news all over town. I won't be long."

Alone, Gil Yeager dropped into a chair, loose and sprawled. For so long he'd been carrying a deep weariness, product of a driving race against time and distance. And he was still whipped with the knowledge that this thing was far from finished and that no real rest would be his until it was. Yet, for the moment at least, here was sanctuary, where he might lie back and let some of the tensions flow out of him.

Good to his promise, Johnny Hock was soon returned and calling softly at the door. Yeager turned the key and let him in. Johnny carried a covered tray. He lowered it to the desk.

"All yours, my friend. Dig in!"

There was a big bowl of savory stew, several thick slices of bread, a generous wedge of pie and a jug of hot coffee. Though his hands trembled with a famished eagerness, Yeager ate slowly, and as the much needed nourishment began to take hold, he steadied and relaxed, and the lines of his face softened and lost some of their harshness. Finished, he pushed back from the desk and searched his pockets for smoking, but without success. He looked at Johnny Hock and shrugged.

"That's how flat I am, John. Not even the price of a sack of tobacco in my jeans. A man on the dodge gets that way."

Johnny Hock indicated a desk drawer. "Caddy of Durham in there. Help yourself."

Yeager did so, and when he had a cigarette rolled and alight, he got to his feet, put his arms above his head and stretched mightily.

"Better. Just a hell of a lot better! When hunger is a raw misery in a man, John, then a solid meal can loom as just about the most important thing in the world."

"And after grub and a smoke, it's sleep for anyone who looks as fagged as you," Johnny Hock said. "There's a bedroll in the back room. Go turn in. Come morning we'll talk things over some more."

"Morning!" exclaimed Yeager. "No, John, not morning. Tonight. I got to see Judge Carmody. Can you get him down here?"

"Probably—if I can make him understand how important it is."

Yeager came swiftly around, the line of his jaw pulling taut. "Tell him it's as important as a man's good name and his liberty; as his right to walk among other men, free, and with a cleared record. Tell him that, John."

"He can be a stubborn, crotchety old pelican, Gil," Johnny Hock said gravely. "It will take more than just your given word to convince him."

"I got more," Yeager said. "I got a lot more than that."

"Then I'll get him down here," Johnny Hock promised. "I'll get him if I have to hog-tie him and lug him over my shoulder."

"Fine! Now, how's for that gun?"

"What do you want it for?"

"To round up Kline Hyatt and bring him here. I want him in on this, too."

Johnny Hock went into another of the desk drawers and came up with a heavy calibered six shooter. He handed it over with a shade of reluctance.

"I fresh loaded it just last week. You won't run wild, will you?"

Yeager hefted the gun, then shoved it down inside the waist band of his faded, ragged jeans.

"No wilder than it takes to make Kline Hyatt stand still while Judge Carmody hears the truth of things. Quit worrying. I got everything figured." As he moved toward the door another thought came to him, and he paused. "Does Hyatt check in at his office at regular intervals like he used to?"

"Most generally."

"Good enough. Well, go get the Judge."

"And you," Johnny Hock cautioned, "you keep an eye out for Ollie Ladd, even more than you do for Kline Hyatt. For when you clubbed Ollie down during your jail-break, you made considerable of a fool of him. You left him with a large-sized hate which he'll nurse forever, him being the sort he is. He's made talk of what he'd do to you, should he ever meet up with you again."

"Ollie Ladd," Yeager said, "is a big, dumb ox."

"That he is," Johnny Hock agreed. "A big, dumb, cruel animal. But just as unpredictable and dangerous as one. And while he may pack a deputy badge out of Kline Hyatt's office, he is first and last a cattle-combine man. So you watch out for him, for he could come up tough."

From the doorway, Yeager showed a hard, mirthless grin.

"I said that a man on the dodge never gathers much in the way of money, John. I forgot to add that he does take on a thick rind of callus. So, if you want to see what another tough one looks like, consider me. See you soon!"

He stepped out into the night and moved slowly along, pausing every little way to look around and renew acquaintance with this town of Tuscarora. Stimulated by the meal he'd just finished, he felt strong and solid and sure of himself, with all his senses sharp and alert.

Flowing in from the east where the burly mass of Sheridan Peak loomed black against the star glitter, a thin, keen wind laid chill breath across the town, and Yeager put his face to it with eager content. Yonder, lights shone in the Elite eating house and in Jake Dolwig's Lodgepole Bar. But George Clyte's barbershop and Barney Flood's leather store were dark, and Yeager had to send his seeking glance as far as the Summit House Hotel before meeting further illumination.

On this side of the street and opposite the Summit House, the square, two-storied bulk of the courthouse lifted, dark from basement to roof. But closer at hand, Patch Kelly's store was aglow, as was a long, low-fronted structure standing midway between store and courthouse.

This was a new one to Yeager, and as he pondered the nature of the place a file of riders whipped into town and hauled to a dust-scattering halt in front of it. They left their saddles and pushed and jostled about the entrance, their voices laying a sharp and echoing eagerness along the street.

His cigarette dead, Yeager tossed the butt aside and started past Kelly's, the habit of wariness he'd acquired causing him to wheel out into the street, and so move beyond the reach of the lights. Abruptly he stopped and turned back. Wise as it was to avoid general recognition until this night's important business was done with, damned if he was going to slink in the shadows forever!

So he went along the walk and was just short of the store's open door when two people stepped from it, to pause for a moment in the flare of light. A clear glimpse of one of them made Yeager whirl close against the store front and lose himself in the darkness there.

Laurie Benedict!

Her head was turned, her face to the light as she smiled at what her companion was saying. Her hair lay smooth and glossy about her head, and the curve of her chin and throat was as faultless and lovely a line as ever.

Laurie Benedict!

Her companion, a compactly built, lithe moving man, was a stranger in Yeager's eyes. Though his face was partially in shadow, Yeager got the impression of an aquiline cast of fea-

8

ture and a glint of white teeth as a low voiced remark ran off into a light laugh.

The pair sauntered away up street and across to the Summit House, there pausing for a moment in the lights of the porch. After which Laurie entered the hotel, while the man came back through the darkness of the street and turned in at the door of the new building. Passing the place a few moments later, Yeager read the sign painted in flowing scroll across a front window. The Golden Horn. Beyond that window sounded the murmur of men's voices and the occasional lift of their laughter.

Yeager prowled on to the courthouse, restless over the surge of feeling that had whipped through him at sight of Laurie Benedict. For he'd come to believe that the past year of hardship and danger and bitterness had knocked all capacity for sentiment and softer emotion out of him, and now, to find otherwise, gave him a stir of unease.

He paused for another careful look around. Beside him lifted the stairs to the wide front gallery and main floor of the courthouse. Directly at hand a door opened into a hallway which ran the full length of the basement to the jail in the rear. A dozen feet along the hall a side door marked the office of sheriff, and this was the door Yeager sought and turned through. Surrounded by silence he felt his way to a far corner and there hunkered down. He laid Johnny Hock's gun on the floor beside him and settled himself to the wait.

Here it was Stygian dark and he had to rely on his ears alone to bring him word of the night and what it held. Over the space of a slow half hour there was little enough. Twice, jogging hoofs was a low mutter of sound along the street, and once a man's shout, wild and exuberant with whiskey, echoed across the night, setting a dog to barking fitfully at the far edge of town. Close at hand, within the wall, mice gnawed and gave off their minute squeaking.

Plagued with restlessness, Yeager was anxious to get on with this thing. Because it would aid greatly, if managed, he was gambling on surprise. He was gambling also on the

9

habits of a man, Sheriff Kline Hyatt. Yet it was quite possible that Hyatt would not show at his office again this night, or it could be Deputy Ollie Ladd who would check the rounds. If either of these strong possibilities occurred, immediate plans would have to be changed and other moves decided on.

Deep sunk in such conjecture and speculation, Yeager missed the sound of approach until footsteps were in the hall and close to the door of the office. Swiftly and silently he scooped up the gun and pushed erect.

A man came into the room, coughing drily. A cigar's lighted tip was a ruby eye in the blackness and the breath of it a swift-spreading acridity. A match snapped and a lamp chimney chimed softly when lifted from its metal bracket. The wick flamed, steadied and grew strong as the chimney was replaced.

In the revealing glow, Sheriff Kline Hyatt stood a lank, round-shouldered man, with a face that was long and tight drawn, and like his small, bleached eyes, full of a sour man's habitual calculating skepticism. For a moment he stood, unaware of another presence in the room. Then he caught the lean shadow of Gil Yeager in the far corner and he came swiftly around. Yeager put Johnny Hock's gun on him.

"Just as you are, Hyatt!"

Recognition flared in Hyatt's eyes and surprise held him as Yeager moved in to lift away his shoulder gun. This, Yeager dropped on the floor and kicked under the desk. Then he tipped a directing head.

"You can douse that lamp again, Hyatt. You and me, we're off for a talk with the right people. Go on, put the light out!"

Instead of obeying, Hyatt spoke with nasal thinness.

"I don't know what you're figuring on, Yeager, but whatever it is, you can't get away with it. I'm putting you under arrest and taking your gun."

Yeager's laugh was a short, harsh bark.

"Like hell you are!"

"I'm arresting you," Hyatt insisted. "Give me that gun!" He reached for it.

A sudden twisting tightened Yeager's lips and his eyes went smoky dark. He cuffed aside Hyatt's reaching hand and jammed the open palm of his own left hard into Hyatt's face, ruining his cigar and snapping back his head. There was enough behind the half-blow, half-push to spin Hyatt and drop him into the desk chair, where he stayed, half-dazed, a faint stain of crimson seeping across his lip. Standing over him, Yeager's words fell bleakly.

"Maybe you understand now, Hyatt. You'd better, because for the past year I've been living like a damned pariah, skulking in dark corners and out in the brush, sleeping with one eye open like any other hunted animal. Yeah, I've had a pretty rough year, Hyatt, because of you and others like you, and if you think it sweetened me up where you're concerned, you couldn't be further wrong. So, get this! I didn't come back to let you lock me up again. I came back to reclaim a number of things that are mine, and whatever I have to do to make good those claims—that I will do!"

He locked a hand in Kline Hyatt's shirt front and hauled him erect.

"You and me, we're off to Johnny Hock's office—by the back way. Kill that light!"

Sour skeptic that he was, Kline Hyatt was no coward. Neither, however, was he a fool. So now, as he met the boring impact of Gil Yeager's bitter regard and found in it no slightest trace of bluff or mercy, he bowed to the inevitable.

Leaning, he cupped a hand above the lamp chimney and blew out the flame. Then, with Yeager in close attendance, and a jabbing gun muzzle a constantly reminding pressure under his short ribs, Sheriff Kline Hyatt moved out of his office and along the hall and so into the night.

2.

JUDGE TERENCE CARMODY was a waspy little man whose head, because of the shaggy mane of white hair covering it, appeared too large for his body. His face was lined and leathery, gnome-like, but from beneath a pair of frosty brows a pair of flashing, electric-blue eyes peered out, to challenge all the injustice in the world. Crotchety, and of short patience, he nevertheless was a completely sound and fair man.

To anyone hearing it for the first time his voice was startling, rolling rich and deep as it did out of that meager body. A wife-beating Indian who once stood in Terence Carmody's court and received a highly vitriolic verbal chastisement, was later heard to mumble awedly about "big thunder in small cloud." In any event, when Judge Carmody chose to speak his official mind, other men listened and were guided thereby.

The muted echo of that thunder was rumbling in Johnny Hock's office as Gil Yeager and Kline Hyatt approached. Hyatt's step dragged with sudden reluctance.

"Judge Carmody is in there."

"That's right," Yeager rapped bluntly. "What's the matter—are you afraid to face him?"

At Yeager's knock, Johnny Hock opened the door and Yeager herded his man through. Judge Carmody had perched himself on a corner of Johnny Hock's desk, but now, letting out a startled growl, he slid free of the desk and stood with his feet spread and his shaggy head thrust forward. He boomed indignant demand.

"What the devil is this? Sheriff Hyatt, who is this man? What's he doing with that gun?"

It was Yeager who answered. "I'm asking you to bear with me, Judge. There's a great deal at stake. This may look a little irregular, but I promise you—"

"Irregular!" exploded the Judge. "That, sir, is a damned mild word to explain such an exhibition. Who are you?"

"The name is Yeager, Gil Yeager."

"Yeager, eh!" snapped the Judge. "In the records of my court it is written that a man of such name broke jail and fled justice."

"I am that man," admitted Yeager steadily. "But it was injustice I fled, not justice."

Judge Carmody wasn't listening. The fiery little jurist had turned on Johnny Hock and was lashing at him furiously.

"So this is why you brought me down here, John Hock! You said—"

"I know what I said," cut in Johnny Hock calmly. "I asked you to meet a friend of mine and hear what he had to say for himself. So why not quit whooping and ranting and listen for a change."

"I'll not listen to, nor have anything to do with any felon beyond my official capacity or outside my official chambers," stormed Judge Terence Carmody. "You hear me, John Hock—nothing at all!"

Towering above him, Johnny Hock dropped a soothing hand on the Judge's shoulder.

"Terence, we've been friends for a long time. You know me about as well as one man can know another. Now do you really believe I'd ask you here under these conditions unless I was convinced an innocent man had been wrongfully accused and prosecuted?"

"And do you realize," sputtered the Judge, "that when you imply a man was mistreated of his rights in my court, you are casting an aspersion on that court—on the integrity of it?"

"Nothing of the sort," denied Johnny Hock. "When Gil Yeager was being tried, you were in Denver on long official leave, testifying for the Government on some railroad subsidy mess. Here, in your court, Judge Elias Blackmur was sitting in your stead. And you know what has happened to Blackmur since then."

"Well, yes," admitted Judge Carmody, a trifle less militantly. "He's turned out to be somewhat of a scoundrel, and stands suspended by the Territorial Governor, awaiting further investigation and possible prosecution for collusion with certain powerful land and cattle interests."

"Exactly!" Johnny Hock emphasized. "So, considering such, are you still unwilling to listen to my good friend, Gil Yeager, and hear what he has to say in his own behalf?"

Carmody turned and laid a fiercely probing regard on Yeager, who met the glance and held it steadily. Finally the Judge nodded, stiffly.

"Very well, I'll listen. But never in the presence of a threatening weapon. Put that gun away, sir!"

"Gladly," Yeager said, laying the weapon on the desk. "Sorry I had to use it to keep Sheriff Hyatt quiet."

Kline Hyatt, physically still, now gave out with sullen verbal complaint.

"Judge, this fellow Yeager has no lawful right to speak with you like this. He's a wanted man."

Judge Carmody lifted a dissenting hand.

"I have said I would listen, and I shall. There are times when extraordinary circumstances demand extraordinary consideration. This could be one of such. We shall see. Very well, Mister Yeager, what is it you wish to say?"

From the front of his shirt, Yeager produced a stained and battered envelope of legal size, and handed it over.

"It's in here, Judge. All of it. Read it."

Lips pursed, eyes pinched in a shadowed frown, Judge Terence Carmody removed the enclosure, unfolded it carefully, and as carefully perused it. Finished with one reading, he went over it a second time. After which he lifted his head and looked around, gravely sober.

"This, gentlemen," he said slowly, "is a startling document.

For the benefit and information of all, it should be read aloud.
That I will now do." He cleared his throat.

" 'To Whom It May Concern:

" 'Be advised that in my presence this day, July 19,
1887, one Emmett Jackson, alias Shad Emmett, did con-
fess to having brought false witness against one Gilman
Yeager, who, in court of law, stood wrongfully and un-
justly charged with murder. Therefore, said Emmett
Jackson, alias Shad Emmett, of his own free will and in
no way unduly coerced, did solemnly swear to the following statement of fact.

" 'That on the day and at the approximate hour one
Cress Lucas was shot to death at a spot on the Summit
Prairie range known as Burnt Corral, he, Emmett Jackson, alias Shad Emmett, did trade talk and tobacco with
said Gilman Yeager along the upper reaches of Aspen
Creek, a vicinity fully twenty miles distant from Burnt
Corral by shortest possible route, this fact making it im-
possible for Gilman Yeager to have been at the scene of
the shooting of Cress Lucas at the time of the crime's
commitment, and so in no way guilty thereof.

" 'In support of this statement, and convinced of its
truthfulness, I hereby give my hand and the seal of my
authority.

" '*Signed:*   Andrew W. MacLeod
" 'United States Marshal' "

When Judge Carmody finished reading, Johnny Hock let
go a deep sigh of relief and looked at Gil Yeager.

"Man—I was just a little scared! I thought maybe you had
us both way out on a long, long limb. But you didn't. And
everything is all right, now."

Kline Hyatt, narrow cheeks pulled to a sour scowling,
spoke up.

"Sounds almost too smooth. Yeager could have paid some
slick lawyer to fake that for him."

"Ridiculous!" snorted Judge Carmody. "Any suggestion of doubt of the authenticity of this document is sheer stupidity. For it happens that I know Andy MacLeod, and have for years. I have corresponded with him, both privately and officially, on numerous occasions. I recognize his hand and his signature. This document is an honest statement of fact. Else Andy MacLeod would never have penned it and put his name to it."

"But why should Shad Emmett have admitted to perjury?" argued Hyatt stubbornly. "What did he have to gain?"

"Something like this, I think," put in Yeager. "Actually, Shad Emmett never did have anything against me personally. And when I came up with him it was in Two Rivers, and he was in custody of Marshal MacLeod, about to take stage for Grand City to answer there on an old train and mail robbery charge. Evidently he figured that it might gain him some degree of leniency in the Grand City court, if he cleared things up for me."

"Right!" agreed Judge Carmody. "Such has occurred in my own court, a man admitting to past misdeed in hope of gaining lighter punishment for the one presently charged with. I take it, Mr. Yeager, that Shad Emmett—or whatever his true name is—withheld this sworn evidence at your trial?"

Yeager nodded. "He was the one person who could prove I was miles away from Burnt Corral when Cress Lucas was killed there. But by the time he reached the witness stand, someone had got to him—evidently with money. Anyhow, he testified that he had not seen me on Aspen Creek as I claimed. After that, as I saw it, my only hope was to break jail, locate Shad Emmett and somehow get the truth out of him. It was a long and desperate chance, and more than once I figured it hadn't done me any good. But I got lucky, finally."

Judge Carmody stared across the room with musing, speculative glance before speaking slowly.

"Mr. Yeager, even the most venal of courts would hardly dare bring a murder charge against a man, based on evidence which appears to have been entirely circumstantial, unless there had occurred some previous display of bad blood between this man and his claimed victim. Was such the case with you?"

Again Yeager nodded. "Yes, Judge, it was. Cress Lucas and me, we'd done some heavy arguing over a range boundary, and one time in the Lodgepole Bar we'd mixed it with our fists and traded some pretty strong talk, as men will when their minds are cluttered with anger. It was common knowledge that Lucas and I were hardly the best of friends." He paused, hesitating, then asked, "What's ahead for me now, Judge?"

"Exoneration, of course," stated Judge Carmody crisply. "Full and complete. No honest court could hesitate in granting you all of that in the face of such a documented alibi as I hold here. I will have the charges against you set aside immediately."

"I'm still not entirely satisfied," Kline Hyatt persisted thinly. "I think further investigation—"

Judge Carmody whirled on him testily.

"Don't persist in playing the utter jackass, Sheriff Hyatt! In a moment you'll have me suspecting personal bias on your part, rather than official assiduity." The Judge's blue eyes were flashing and the thunder rolling in his tone. "As of this moment, you will consider yourself officially advised that Gilman Yeager stands completely cleared of all past charges. You understand that, and will be guided accordingly?"

Hyatt nodded sulkily. "I'm remembering that in making his jail break, Yeager assaulted my deputy. And that he threw a gun on me to force me over here from my office. Does he go clear on those two points?"

"In view of the gross miscarriage of justice which he was correcting, I think both instances may be viewed as excusable. That should be all, Sheriff."

Kline Hyatt turned toward the door, but Gil Yeager stopped him.

"Just a minute! Judge, I'd like you to pass opinion on another little matter."

Frowning, the Judge peered at Yeager. "And what is that?"

"Money. Four hundred and fifty-five dollars and a few odd cents. I'll settle for an even four hundred and fifty. I had that much in my jeans at the time of my arrest and it was taken away from me. I want it back. I really need it, as you can see." Yeager indicated his all too apparent raggedness.

"Consider me witness to the fact that Gil had the money, Terence," put in Johnny Hock solidly. "I know, because I gave it to him. It was money left with me by Lyle Detwiler, who owed it to Gil on a cattle deal."

Judge Carmody put his glance on Kline Hyatt again. "What have you to say to that, Sheriff?"

Hyatt shrugged. "He'll get the money, of course. I'm no damned thief. In any major arrest we always empty the prisoner's pockets and hold what's in them for future court disposition."

Yeager said, "I'll be around first thing in the morning to collect, Hyatt."

Johnny Hock unlocked the door and Kline Hyatt moved off into the night.

Judge Terence Carmody pushed a hand through his snowy thatch.

"This," he remarked slowly, "has been something new in my judicial experience. A most unusual evening."

"All of that!" agreed Johnny Hock emphatically. "And as such, calls for a little something to settle a man's nerves. You'll join Gil and me in one?"

"Why now," the Judge said with alacrity, "I don't mind if I do. The righting of an injustice should ever be cause for a moment of celebration."

Johnny Hock produced bottle and glasses from a corner cupboard. Judge Carmody took his neat, but shook his head when Johnny would have poured another.

"Thanks, John—but no." The sternness in the Judge's eyes

had become a merry twinkle. "While Mrs. Carmody does not object to one, she never approves of two. And when she sets her mind to a bit of cross examination she never fails at dredging up the truth." He turned to Gil Yeager. "I will need this document to record. After which it will be returned to you. I congratulate you, sir, on your exoneration, and rejoice with you because of it. And now, gentlemen, if you'll excuse me . . . ?"

When the door closed behind the doughty little jurist, Yeager looked at Johnny Hock and grinned wearily.

"That tough little rooster! The pair of you, John, have restored some of my faith in human nature. I hope you understand how deeply I'm thanking you?"

Johnny Hock waved a deprecatory hand. "Just so long as it came out right. Now, what's next for you?"

Yeager stretched and yawned until his jaws cracked.

"That bedroll you mentioned a while back. With the big pressure off, I'm dead for sleep."

Johnny Hock poured another drink. "And tomorrow?"

Some of the tired ease that had settled over Yeager's face drained away, replaced by the shadow of a tightlipped harshness.

"Ah, yes—tomorrow! Well, my friend, tomorrow I begin reclaiming all that is mine."

"Meaning maybe range—cattle?"

"Meaning exactly that, John. Every acre, every head."

Johnny Hock drove the bottle cork home with a smack of his open palm and spoke gravely.

"That will not be easy, Gil. The land and cattle combine is stronger today than it was a year ago, if for no other reason than the opposition is scattered and weakened and dispirited. A year ago it was strong enough to corrupt a court and come close to hanging you. It was a tough outfit then, when Brick Rand was bossing it, and in my opinion Rand was an upright, kind hearted gentleman along side of this new fellow, this Meade Bastian. Also, Kline Hyatt is playing his usual politician's game of stringing along with the strong side. You'll get no help from his office."

"Wasn't counting on any," Yeager said. "You ever see anything of Jed Mims?"

"Occasionally."

"What's he doing?"

"Odd-jobbing when he can for one of the old outfits. But things are bad with them. Hans Ogaard went bust and left the country. From all accounts, old Alec Trezevant is about washed up, too. Gene Hickerson and Pete Blalock and Jack Swayze are still hanging on, but barely. Harry Plume is in fair shape, but he's such a damned skinflint he can get by where better men starve. And that's what the Chinkapin country is, as you know—starvation range."

Yeager considered a moment, brooding. "You think there's any fight left in those fellows, John?"

Johnny Hock located a pipe in a desk drawer, packed and lit it and stared into the smoke.

"Six or eight months ago, maybe. Now, I don't know. It's—well—ah—"

"Go ahead, say it," cut in Yeager quietly. "They feel that I let them down, once. Maybe I did. But a man can change, can't he?"

"Sure, sure." Johnny Hock let out another mouthful of smoke and fanned it aside with his hand. "Gil, I'm not out to try and tell you your business. But I just can't see you with a chance of winning any fight against that combine. You haven't the money to stand up to a lot of court litigation, and the combine is just plain too damn big and powerful for you or any other lone man to do any good against it physically."

Yeager took a prowling turn about the room. "What would you have me do—forfeit range and cattle rightfully mine? Take what amounts to ten good years of my life and hand it free to that flock of damned thieves? Try and make a new start somewhere else, all at loose ends? You'd have me do that, John?"

"Even so it would be better than wasting the rest of your life in a fight you can't win," Johnny Hock said bluntly. "But I'm not suggesting you make a new start at loose ends. I got something figured for you, Gil. Like this. Walt Haley, over in Gardnerville, wants to sell his freighting business. I'm plenty interested, because his routes would tie in well with my present ones, and I'm leaving early tomorrow for Gardnerville to close the deal. It is something that will surely go for anyone who will leave the bottle alone and tend to business; that's been Walt's trouble—he's just too fond of the bottle. I've been wondering where I'd find the right man to put in there, and you've shown up just in time. The job's yours on a partnership basis, Gil."

"But I'm cattle, John," protested Yeager. "I don't know anything about running a freight line."

"All it takes is common sense and a willingness to stay sober." Johnny Hock put a freshening match across the bowl of his pipe, his lips smacking softly as he puffed. "Furthermore, you'll be playing a sure winning game instead of a losing one."

Yeager took another turn up and down the room, face dark with frowning thought. Presently he paused and regarded Johnny Hock levelly.

"That's mighty generous and about what I'd expect of you, John. But I got to say—no. For the past year I've been running away, running and dodging and skulking. I had no choice, as you know. But I got awful damned tired of that sort of thing and I promised myself that if I ever managed to clear my name, then I'd never run again, not from anyone or anything. And if I took you up on this offer, that's exactly what I'd be doing, once more running away. So, win or lose, I'm going to make a fight of it."

Into Yeager's eyes came a look of far away speculation. A tautness touched his face, accenting the gaunt, hard jut of his jaw and cheekbones. Slowly he went on.

"Maybe it will be a lone-handed fight. More than likely it will be. Still I'm going to make it. For while a fair amount of ease and certainty is good for a man, there should be more to his makeup than just a willingness to settle for such. Hell! He's got to prove something or other in this world, if for no other reason than to justify his brief walk across it. And the only way I can prove anything is to put up a fight for what is rightfully mine. So, while I'm thanking you again, John—that is the way it has to be."

Johnny Hock sighed and hunched his shoulders. "Was afraid you'd feel so. You're a lot different man than you were a year ago, Gil. I see a darkness in you now that was not there before."

"Toward my enemies, probably," Yeager admitted readily. "But toward my good friends—never!" He dropped a hand on Johnny Hock's arm and a swift smile warmed and softened his face.

Meeting the look, Johnny Hock nodded resignedly.

"Every man has his own trail to travel, and to make it worthwhile to him, I suppose he's got to go it his own way. I'd have you remember one thing, Gil. While I honestly feel you've damn little chance of winning, I'll still be in there helping any way I can. Don't you ever forget that! Now go turn in. You're out on your feet."

3.

LEAVING THE ELITE and angling up street toward the courthouse, Gil Yeager moved through the blaze of a newly risen sun. A night of sound sleep, breakfast at the counter of the Elite warm under his belt, the good taste of a final cup of coffee lingering on his tongue along with the flavor of the day's first cigarette—all combined to give him a sense of well-being he hadn't known in many, many months.

Patch Kelly, just opening his store, threw a brief glance, then hurriedly straightened.

"I will be damned! Gil Yeager!" He looked anxiously up and down street. "Man—get out of sight!"

Yeager grinned at him. "No need, Patch. Thanks for the kind thought, though. I'll be around a little later to spend some money with you."

He went on, leaving Patch staring and wondering.

At the Golden Horn both doors were latched back and a swamper wielded a busy broom about the entrance. Standing in the clear sunlight, watching this activity, was a man in a dark suit, a slim perfecto burning between his teeth. Out of the open doors leaked the breath of last night's accumulated activities; stale tobacco smoke, the sour-sweet reek of whiskey, and the many odors of the flesh which lusty men leave behind them.

No attention was paid Yeager until he was within a yard of passing. Then the cigar smoker's head lifted, showing a face pale and smooth and expressionless. Also a pair of the blackest eyes Yeager had ever seen in a human. Obsidian black, and just as hard and unrevealing. For a long moment the flinty scrutiny held, and Yeager felt he was being evaluated, catalogued and filed away. Then the black eyes slid aside and their owner was once again an entirely neutral and retiring figure.

From the sharp angled shadow of the courthouse steps, Deputy Sheriff Ollie Ladd watched Gil Yeager approach. A formidable figure of a man, the deputy's regard was frankly hating. Meeting the look and knowing the thought behind it, Yeager paused and gave it back, stare for stare. He tipped his head.

"Hyatt inside?"

"He's in there." Ollie Ladd's grudging answer rolled out thick and surly and guttural.

Yeager looked him up and down. "Time's been known to sweeten some things. Not you though, eh Ollie?"

Ollie's broad and heavy lips lifted at one corner in something not far from a soundless snarl. Beyond that, nothing.

"Suppose we go in?" Yeager suggested.

"Maybe I like it here," retorted Ollie.

"I got things to say," Yeager told him coldly. "Things you should listen to, for they could save you future trouble."

Ollie Ladd hesitated, then shrugged and wheeled through the door beside him. He tramped ponderously along the hallway and turned in at Hyatt's office, Gil Yeager following.

Kline Hyatt sat at his desk, chewing a ragged cigar, looking as sour and indrawn as usual. In front of him lay a little pile of currency and some few odd coins. He met Yeager's glance briefly, then indicated the money.

"Count it."

"I intend to." Yeager showed a hard, mocking grin, then drawled, "For I just can't bring myself to trust you any more, Hyatt."

Kline Hyatt removed the cigar from his lips, spat a remnant of tobacco into the sawdust box beside the desk.

"You've had a little run of luck, Yeager. Don't try and stretch it!"

Yeager riffled through the currency, then gathered up the coins, one by one. He nodded.

"Four hundred and fifty-five dollars and eighty cents. The exact amount. I'm surprised you remembered so well. I'm also surprised you hadn't spent this, months ago."

Hyatt stirred restlessly, his words running more thinly nasal than ever.

"I said—watch it! You can just easy as hell stir yourself up another jag of trouble."

Apparently not listening, Yeager wadded the currency into one ragged pocket and dumped the silver into another. This done, however, he slapped a hard palm on the desk top and leaned across it, and now there was no lightness in his voice at all.

"You're the one to watch it, Hyatt! For you're not looking at the same man you helped push around a year ago. I'd have thought you'd realized that last night. No, not the same man at all. That fellow was an easy-going, trustful sort. Different now, though. He's no longer one of the meek of the earth, no longer a fool sheep, fat for the shearing. Pay you to remember that, Hyatt."

Straightening, he came around, stepped close to Ollie Ladd and jabbed a stiff forefinger against Ollie's burly chest.

"You too, Ollie. I understand you've been making strong talk of what you intended doing to me, should I ever show in these parts again. That wasn't wise. For here I am and any time I might get the idea of calling you. Then, where would you be?"

He moved to the door, that hard mockery pulling at his lips again.

"You've no idea how I've looked forward to this—a chance to tell off the pair of you. Now it's done, I feel I'm a whole man again."

He went out.

Ollie Ladd began to curse heavily, but Kline Hyatt flagged him to silence again with a curt hand.

"No point in that. Doesn't do a lick of good. We just got to take it and like it."

"Not here," blurted Ollie. "I don't like it and I won't take it."

"You'll damn well take it if you expect to go on wearing that star," Hyatt snapped. He threw the dead butt of his cigar into the sawdust box, took a fresh one from a vest pocket and lit it. "This office," he went on between puffs, "is going to play its cards a little more careful for a while."

"But we can't afford to let him face us down this way," Ollie argued. "I still say we should slap an arrest on him, lock him up again."

Kline Hyatt considered his deputy with open exasperation and spoke acidly.

"Can't you get it through your head that Yeager now stands cleared of any and all charges? I told you Judge Carmody was seeing to that."

25

For some little time Ollie Ladd considered this, scowl wrinkles fanning from the corners of his eyes, heavy jaw and lower lip outthrust. In Ollie there lay a wide disparity between brain and brawn. Mainly, he functioned only to the uncertain guidance of his native wild instincts and desires. He stood a hulking, brooding figure, unpredictable and dangerous.

"You talked back tough to Yeager just now," he reminded presently. "You told him to watch himself, else he'd hatch more trouble. How about that?"

Hyatt shrugged. "A man gives you the elbow, you give it back. Five minutes later he's more or less forgotten, and so have you."

"Not me," growled Ollie stubbornly. "I don't forget that easy."

Hyatt showed his acid weariness again.

"You miss the point, Ollie. Before we look out for anybody else, we look out for ourselves. This office is politics, which makes us politicians. And a smart politician trims his sails to the need of the moment. He knows when to swing one way, when to swing another. Also, which is even more important, when to hold the middle course until he's sure which way the wind is really going to blow. For the present, at least, that's the course this office is taking. Right down the middle!"

"Meade Bastian and Duke Royale, maybe they won't like that," Ollie said.

Kline Hyatt stared into the smoke of his cigar, scowling a little. He shrugged.

"For the present, they'll have to."

Lying back in George Clyte's chair, Gil Yeager savored fully the unaccustomed luxury of a barber's ministrations. The past hour he'd spent soaking in the tub in Clyte's back room, and he was now dressed in clothes new and fresh from Patch Kelly's shelves. As Clyte finished with him and he stepped from the chair, he seemed to have shed years along with what the shears and razor had removed. He surveyed himself in the wall mirror and turned to Clyte, thin amusement on his face.

"George, who is this fellow? It's so long since I had a good look at him, I hardly recognize him. What's the tariff?"

Clyte named it and Yeager paid.

"What about your old clothes?" Clyte asked.

Yeager laid down another quarter. "Get somebody to burn 'em. Hire a strong man, else they'll walk right away from him."

He went out into the brightness of mid-morning and had his second good look at this town of Tuscarora. Some life was on the street. Three saddle mounts stood at the hitch rail of the Golden Horn, while a single one dozed before the Lodgepole Bar. A spring wagon was drawn up in front of Kelly's store, and now the owner appeared, climbed to the seat and rolled slowly out of town, the shuffling jog of his ancient team stirring up a small banner of dust.

Up street, Ollie Ladd came away from the courthouse and moved along as far as the Golden Horn, where he started to turn in. Spying Yeager, he paused and stood staring. For a long half minute this dark and unreadable situation held, before Ollie wheeled into the barroom.

A thread of tension crawled up Gil Yeager's spine, chilling out some of his new-found sense of well-being. No man, he reflected soberly, could be entirely sure of what was stirring in the murky recesses of Ollie Ladd's mind, nor what wild impulse might govern his mood at any time. One thing, however, could be surely counted on. Once Ollie Ladd hated, it was for all time.

The relaxed ease faded from Yeager's face and he crossed to Patch Kelly's store. Patch looked him up and down.

"The clothes seem to fit all right. Or did you forget something?"

"Not forgotten, Patch. Just something I had to think about, and I've done my thinking. What you got on the gun rack?"

Lips pursed, the storekeeper considered him soberly.

27

"Now it is my business to sell folks what they want to buy. But just now, Gil Yeager, I'm not sure I want to sell. I'd not like seeing you in trouble again."

"Patch," said Yeager, "it comes to me that the only way I could stay free of trouble on Summit Prairie, would be to take my foot in my hand and run. Well, I'm not going to run. I didn't come back here to run. So—let's have a look at those guns!"

Patch Kelly turned up his hands, jerked his head toward the rack. "Your business."

There were several rifles. Yeager decided on a Model '73 Winchester, caliber .44-40. After which he looked over half a dozen sixshooters before choosing a Colt gun to handle the same cartridge. He bought a saddle boot for the rifle and a belt and holster for the Colt. He found some rags, perched himself on the end of the counter and began cleaning the factory grease from the weapons.

Patch Kelly, rotund and ruddy, watched with shrewd Irish eyes. He shook his head.

"I still don't like it, my friend. The Gil Yeager I used to know was hardly what you'd call a gunman. Which was one big reason I never did believe he killed Cress Lucas."

Yeager paused in his cleaning chore while he spun up a smoke.

"Obliged for that kind thought, Patch," he remarked drily. "The Gil Yeager you used to know was a safe and sane, trustful damn fool. But that Gil Yeager ain't around any more. You still keep a sixshooter in your cash drawer?"

"Sure I do."

"Why?"

"Just a bit of precaution. Stores have been held up, so they tell me."

"Right!" nodded Yeager. "You keep a gun handy, just in case. Well, I've already been robbed, and I know who did it, and I intend getting back everything taken from me, with maybe a little extra for interest. That's it, Patch. That's all of it."

He bent to his chore again.

Out in the street a buckboard rolled to a stop in front of the Summit House. Carrying a small gripsack, Laurie Benedict crossed the hotel porch and climbed to the buckboard seat beside her brother. Burke Benedict showed his sister a quick, fond glance.

"Have a good visit with Maggie Spelle?"

"Yes."

The brevity of the reply and the slightly subdued tone drew another glance.

"Nothing wrong, is there?"

"No. I've some news, though. Gil Yeager is back."

About to kick off the brake and urge his team to movement, Burke Benedict suspended both moves abruptly.

"Gil Yeager! Here—on the prairie?"

Laurie nodded. "That's the word Maggie and I got at breakfast this morning."

"But he'd made a clean getaway," protested Burke. "Why should he risk coming back?"

"It seems that Shad Emmett has confessed to false witness at the trial, so Judge Carmody has declared all charges against Gil struck from the record."

"So that's it!" Burke stared off along the street for a moment. "And now Gil's back—a free man. I wonder what he intends to do? There's nothing left here for him."

"There are the things he once had," Laurie said quickly.

"If you mean range and cattle, where are they?" Burke asked. "I haven't seen a critter packing Gil Yeager's old iron in months and months. And right now there's a good thousand or twelve hundred combine whitefaces ranging Lazy Y grass. What hope could one man have of moving them off and regaining possession? Certainly not Gil Yeager. For as I remember him, he was a great one to play things peaceful and safe and sure."

A short, terse bitterness broke from Laurie. "Have we the right to charge anyone with playing matters safe and sure?"

Slow blood stained Burke's cheeks and something of a trapped weariness showed in his deep eyes.

"Wasn't that hitting a little low, Laurie?"

She was quickly contrite, catching at his arm. "I'm sorry. If only I had just half your patience and goodness of heart—!"

Burke reached over and patted her hand. "You'll do to take along. We've just got to play the cards dealt us the best way we know how."

Again he stared along the street, a rawboned, somber-faced young giant with a kindly mouth, and features moulded to a grave and stubborn patience. He sighed deeply, swung his big shoulders as though to ease them under the pressure of an invisible burden. Then he kicked off the brake, clucked to his team and drove on down street to the rail in front of Kelly's store.

Gil Yeager, finished with the cleaning of his guns, had broken open a box of ammunition and was filling the loops of his gunbelt with the fat, yellow cartridges. At the sound of Burke Benedict's measured, solid step at the store doorway he looked up, saw who was entering, then slid from the counter and stood guardedly watching.

Coming from the outside brightness into the store's shadowy confines, neither Burke nor Laurie Benedict was aware of Yeager's presence. But on moving nearer the counter, Laurie seemed to feel the intentness of his regard, for she stopped short and met his glance with a swift turned head. He touched his hat.

"Hello, Laurie."

Before she could answer, Burke swung around.

"Yeager!" He let it stand that way for a moment, then added in milder tone, "Just heard you were back on the prairie."

A hint of the sardonic showed in Yeager's eyes. "Word does travel. How are things with you, Burke?"

There was that behind the question which made Burke flush slightly. "About the same." He went on swiftly, as though to tender a gesture toward cordiality. "Glad to hear matters have cleared up for you. I don't mind saying I never did think you had anything to do with that Cress Lucas affair."

The sardonic glint in Yeager's eyes deepened. "You should have climbed up on your hind legs a year ago and announced that. It might have helped a lot, then."

Again there was a swift rush of color through Burke Benedict's gaunt cheeks, while a pressure thinned his lips and a flicker of fire showed momentarily in his eyes. Then, much as a badgered bear might have, he shook his head, shrugged, and turned to Patch Kelly and in tight tones began ordering up several items.

As yet, Laurie had not acknowledged Yeager's greeting. Now, with head high and shoulders very straight, she flayed him with the stormiest of glances, her face pale except for a spot of crimson in either cheek. She had the same fine, deep-set eyes as her brother, and now they were blazing, while her lips trembled over scalding words which lay very close to utterance, but which she managed to hold back.

She was, thought Yeager, much the same Laurie Benedict he'd always known. Even in the shadow of her present anger there remained the well-remembered charm of earlier, better days. Her mouth was still the same tender, expressive index to her mood. Anger, tears, happiness, laughter—he'd seen and known them all in her, and he'd suffered under the first and exulted with the last.

Particularly was it easy to recall her laughter. The soft, quick gaiety of it, accompanied always by a little toss of her head. How he used to listen for it! Maybe he was still listening. . . .

It was his turn to shake himself, as though he would be rid of the beginnings of a softer mood of which he was afraid and determined to avoid. Moving to leave, he gathered up his gear and found himself again meeting Laurie's glance. The anger still flared in her eyes, but now it was being curtained by a mist of reproachful tears.

Gruffness climbed into Yeager's throat.

"Sorry," he said. "Sorry, Laurie. But when a dog's been kicked around enough, he gets the snarling habit."

He went out, pausing on the store porch, eyes pinched and dark against the glare of the sun.

Anger was in him, all of it at himself. That damned black temper again. Burke Benedict had never done him any wrong, and he had no just cause to hit out with caustic sarcasm the way he did. Too, he might have known that a slap at Burke was certain to hurt Laurie, for they had always been very close together, had Burke and Laurie Benedict.

The thudding of hoofs along the street jerked Yeager from his dark mood of self-reproach. Four men came riding, one slightly in advance of the rest. This one wore his hat pushed back, and beneath the upturned brim his hair showed rusty red. Sighting Yeager, he threw a swift word across his shoulder to his companions, then spun his horse to a trampling halt at the hitch rail.

"Well, well!" he drawled jeeringly. "If it isn't Mister Yeager himself. They told me you'd shown up again. I wonder why. Would it be to shoot another man in the back?"

Yeager gave the redhead a long, cool stare. Here in front of him sat the man who, more than any other, was responsible for the past year of misery and desperation and fugitive hardship. Such as Kline Hyatt and Ollie Ladd and Shad Emmett and the venal, dishonored Judge Elias Blackmur had merely implemented what this man had schemed and put in motion. They had been the puppets and this fellow the one who had manipulated the strings.

"Brick," Yeager said evenly, "you haven't changed a bit, have you? The same damn liar as always."

The taunting grin on Brick Rand's broad, freckled face stiffened. "You've learned bad habits while away, Yeager. Talking strong, I mean. You're gaunted down some, too. From running far and fast, maybe?"

"Maybe. You notice, though, where I stand now—right back on Summit Prairie. And, while we're noticing this and that, it's plain to see you've been living high. Enjoying good times, eh, Brick—getting fat off what you stole from better men?"

This mocking observation hit sharply home, for the decided beginnings of a paunch hung out over Rand's belt. Rand's grin faded completely.

"You," he said heavily, "are making a damn good start toward another chunk of trouble, Yeager."

Now it was Yeager's laugh which mocked. "You sound just like Kline Hyatt, Brick."

A plan that had been in and out of Yeager's mind several times, now quickened to solid resolve. The element of danger in it was strong, for it meant putting everything on the line, and if it failed it could be his quick finish on Summit Prairie. Yet it was vital that he prove something to all men. And what better time and place than right here and right now where many could listen and observe?

He spat in the dust between Rand and himself, his lips curling. It was a deliberate thing, carrying the broadest of contemptuous insult. His words fell bitingly.

"Yeah, Brick—you always did have a big, loose mouth. I've often wondered if your backbone was as wide as your talk. I'm still wondering."

The redhead stared at him, as though measuring him and trying to guess his purpose. Yeager spat in the dust again.

"Waiting, Brick. And still wondering. How wide—and what color?"

Abruptly a savagely deepening anger rushed through Brick Rand's heavy cheeks, and Yeager saw that he had succeeded in his immediate objective, which was to taunt Rand into a corner he couldn't afford to back out of. For the other riders had heard and observed all, and were beginning to stir impatiently. One of them spoke up harshly.

"He's asking for it, Brick. Either you take him—or I will!"

Rand gave no sign of having heard. He sat very still in his saddle, leaning forward, his hot, pale eyes intent. Once more Gil Yeager used the spurs.

33

"I've heard it said you were a real bucko boy, Brick. What's the matter, gone soft?"

Rand cursed. It was an eruptive, breaking growl in his throat.

"God damn you! Come down here and find out!"

Yeager laid aside his armful of gear, dropped off the porch, ducked under the hitch rail and stood waiting.

"Right with you, Brick. Let's see you get out of that saddle!"

4.

MAKING HIS CHALLENGE, Gil Yeager had stepped even with the head of Brick Rand's horse and a short stride to one side, waiting for Rand to dismount. But Rand did not leave his saddle in a normal manner. Instead he came headlong in a swooping dive. He smashed into Yeager and knocked him off his feet.

The impact was brutal. Where Rand's shoulder took him in the chest, Yeager knew a swift, numbing agony. Yet the very ferocity of his surprise move did Rand not all good, either, for the weight and power behind his lunge carried him over and past Yeager, his face striking hard and grinding in the dust.

Yeager rolled, got his feet under him and pulled erect, swaying and unsteady. In front of him, Rand was also straightening up. The redhead had lost his hat and his hair was splashed and fouled with the street's dust, and he was spitting more of the same from bruised and pouting lips. He glared at Yeager, gathered himself and came ahead, throwing a clubbing punch.

Gil Yeager saw the blow coming, but his reactions were too numbed for him to dodge it. It landed full on the side of his head, knocking him back against the hitch rail, only the support of this keeping him from going down again. He slid his weight along the rail, stumbling, and so retreating, swung past the end of the weathered, use-slickened barrier, putting it between Rand and himself, thus winning a moment in which to regain a measure of strength and balance.

Blindly intent on getting at Yeager, Rand lunged against the rail, which caught him solidly at the belt line, held him short and threw him off balance. He grabbed at the rail to steady himself and this brought both his hands fully down.

Yeager did not miss the opportunity. He rammed a fist into Rand's face, snapping his head back and bringing a gush of crimson from a corner of his mouth. Then, before the redhead could recover, Yeager circled the end of the hitch rail once more and so into the clear of the street, where he waited, reaching deep for air.

Brick Rand came around, pushed a hand across his mashed lips and stared at the smear of crimson which showed. Sight of this set him off again and once more he came on.

This time, Yeager stepped inside a fury driven swing, letting the blow slide harmlessly over his shoulder while he braced himself to meet Rand's rush, chest to chest. For a little time they stayed so, neither giving ground. Then Yeager moved quickly back, set himself, and as Rand came bulling forward, sunk both fists deep into the redhead's body.

This was a thing he had calculated on, even as he had set out to rawhide Brick Rand into action. For the roll of flesh hanging out above Rand's belt had looked soft, and now, as his driving fists dug into it, Gil Yeager found it so.

A gusty grunt broke from Rand. He stopped in his tracks, his eyes dilating and going a little blank. He tried to grab and hold, but Yeager, bleakly merciless, knocked the pawing hands aside and hammered home two more body blows, coming up on his toes to get all he could into the punishing punches.

Now it was a groan which erupted from Rand's throat. He wobbled and began giving ground. Vengefully, Yeager went after him, reached his jaw with one long, winging blow, then cornered him against the hitch rail and savagely pounded him again and again in his shrinking belly.

Rand sagged. He landed a couple of aimless, mauling swings, but there wasn't much behind them now. Yeager brushed them off and beat relentlessly at that quaking midriff.

The redhead began to retch, his mouth open and running crimson slime, his labor for breath a choked gasping. His legs went rubbery and began sliding out from under him. Yeager measured him and smashed him savagely on his loose jaw. Rand's head rolled and he crumpled down.

It had been a short, brutal, thunderous interval, and it had eaten up more physical energy than Gil Yeager realized. For now the world began spinning around and he had to catch at the hitch rail to keep from joining Brick Rand in the dust.

Where Rand's first blow had landed, the side of Yeager's face was numb. His mouth had been cut and the saltiness of his own blood lay on his tongue. His arms hung heavy and he could not get nearly enough air into his aching laboring lungs. Sweat stung and blurred his eyes.

Of a sudden there were horses crowding about and the angry voices of men sawed back and forth above him. Spinning under rough reining a horse slammed into him, knocked him staggering. A stirrup, filled with a rider's boot, swung at him, missed, then hooked back with better aim, and a spur rowel ripped a burning way across his shoulder.

Yeager grabbed blindly at the owner of the spur and hooked his fingers in the fellow's belt. He set back, tried to drag his man from the saddle. But a fist beat at his face and head, driving him off.

Now a shrill yell kited along the street, followed by the flat, hard smash of a gunshot. Again came the biting, menacing yell. The press about Yeager broke and whirled away.

Once more he stood alone and in the clear, pushing a hand across his face, wiping away the fog of exhaustion and punishment. From the dust under the hitch rail, Brick

Rand had struggled up on one elbow, head wobbling, bloody jaw crooked and sagging. A few yards distant, the three riders with Rand were loosely bunched, their attention only slightly on Yeager now. For, limping in across the street came a gaunt, craggy-faced figure in worn jeans and faded shirt and run-over boots: a man who held a Winchester carbine level with his hip and swung the lever of the gun as he jacked a fresh cartridge from magazine to chamber.

Yeager blinked clouded eyes. "Jed!" he croaked. "Jed Mims—!"

"Hiya, boy!" came the answer. "Be with you in a minute."

As harsh of voice as he was of face, Jed Mims now eyed the three riders and challenged one of them bleakly.

"You—Starker! I saw you swing that spur. I saw you try to kick Gil's ribs in, then use a rowel on him. Mebbe I shouldn't have wasted that shot in the air. You want it different, I won't waste the next!" Jed Mims brought the carbine half way to his shoulder.

"Easy, Mims! Easy with that gun!"

It was Sheriff Kline Hyatt who threw this order sharply ahead of him as, along with Ollie Ladd, he came hurrying up. He reached for the carbine, but Jed Mims avoided him.

"No you don't! Run that combine crowd out of here first. Then you can talk to me."

"This thing stops right here," Hyatt emphasized. He put his glance on the three riders. "All right, Starker—you and Jenks and Partridge get out of town!"

Mitch Starker, dark-faced, bull-necked, wanted to argue the point.

"We came with Brick, we stay with him."

"Rand will be taken care of," Hyatt said curtly. "And you're doing as you're told. The three of you—get out of town! I'm not telling you again."

Kline Hyatt came fully around, and abruptly this lank, stooped, sour-faced man of the star seemed to gain in stature, while a current of definite authority rolled along the street. Mitch Starker eyed him sullenly, then switched his glance to put a long stare on Gil Yeager before reining away with the other two. Hyatt watched them for a moment, then turned again to Jed Mims.

"Now I'll take that gun!"

Mims surrendered it. Hyatt jacked the weapon empty, handed it back. "Next time you hit town, leave this thing in your saddle boot."

"That'll depend," Jed Mims retorted sturdily. "I haul this gun with me to suit my needs as they come. Like now. I hear Gil Yeager is back. I ride to town to find out for sure. What do I see? Well, I see Gil, all right. He's tanglin' with Brick Rand, man to man, and takin' mighty good care of him, too. Then what happens? Why, Mitch Starker and them other two try to ride Gil down, to kick him and rowel him. What do you expect me to do, stand still and cheer? Like hell! So I move in. And at my age, when I'm set to take on three at a time, then I'm luggin' along my old carbine."

From an elbow, Brick Rand had struggled to his knees and was now reaching for a grip on the hitchrail. Achieving this, he hauled painfully up, then lay across the rail in another spasm of retching sickness. Kline Hyatt jerked a nod to his deputy.

"Give him a hand, Ollie."

Ollie Ladd took hold of Rand and steered him away on shambling, uncertain feet. Kline Hyatt turned to Gil Yeager.

"What have you to say for yourself? Just because you stand cleared of the old charge doesn't mean you're free to run wild. What set off this row?"

Steadier now, Yeager shrugged. "I'm just leaving Patch Kelly's. Rand and the others come riding. Rand sees me, pulls up and starts throwing the rawhide. I give it back to him. We tangle. Simple as that."

"Just so!" exulted Jed Mims. "And Mister Rand buys himself one first class currying! Gil, that last lick you hit him sounded like you'd broke a board." Approval mounted in the grizzled rider. He gripped Yeager's arm. "Boy, you could stand a mite of cleaning up, and a drink wouldn't hurt you none, either. Come along to Jake Dolwig's and we'll take care of both."

"An idea," Yeager agreed. He looked at Kline Hyatt. "Well?"

"Go on," Hyatt said. "But remember what I told you. You'll get no special privilege from me."

Yeager turned to the store porch for his gear, and for the first time was conscious of the people standing there. Patch Kelly for one. Burke and Laurie Benedict for two more. Patch Kelly wore a small, musing smile and his eyes were snapping bright as though he'd just observed something which set him to considering some not unpleasant speculation of his own. Burke Benedict's look was that of one not too sure he could believe what he'd just witnessed.

As for Laurie Benedict, she was held by a still inscrutability. A slight pallor froze her cheeks and her eyes were big and dark. A grave mystery was in her glance and, meeting it, Yeager tipped his head slightly.

"Some more of the snarling dog, Laurie."

Gathering up his gear, he moved across the street with Jed Mims.

Together with Barney Flood, Jake Dolwig stood at the door of the Lodgepole Bar. They had witnessed the fight and Barney Flood, a wispy little man who smelled eternally of leather, saddle soap and shoemaker's wax, was sputtering excitedly.

"Now there was somethin' I never expected to see—somebody take on Brick Rand in a rough and tumble and cut him down to size so complete. But it happened, by jollies! I know it did, because I seen it!"

Jake Dolwig, face round and smooth and bland, held open the door of the Lodgepole for Yeager and Jed Mims, and his murmur was soft as they passed.

"I enjoyed that. It has been long overdue."

Jed Mims spun a chair into place for Gil Yeager, then called for a bucket of water. Jake Dolwig brought this, along with a clean bar towel. Yeager doused the towel, then held it, wet and cold and greatly comforting to his bruised face. Jed Mims, circling beyond the bar end, brought a glass holding a strong three fingers of whiskey.

"This'll help, boy."

Yeager downed it and the fire in it took hold and spread. He leaned back, letting go a deep, steadying sigh. He looked around, showing the shadow of a twisted grin.

"If anybody is wondering how I did it, I'm wondering a little, myself. All I know is, I took a chance his belly would be as soft as it looked, and I happened to guess right."

"For my money there wasn't anything wrong with the last one you laid on his chin," vowed Jed Mims.

The door of the saloon opened and Ollie Ladd came in, darkly glowering. He placed his forbidding bulk in front of Yeager and growled flat announcement.

"You know what you did, Yeager? You broke Brick Rand's jaw. That's gettin' pretty damned rough."

Yeager blinked. "Broke his jaw!" He lifted his fist and stared at it. "This is all I hit him with."

"No matter. You broke his jaw."

"Well, what of it?" challenged Jed Mims truculently. "It was an even-up, two-man ruckus, wasn't it? Gil was just usin' his two fists against Rand's two. And for that matter, there could be some along Summit Prairie, me included, who wouldn't have wept none if Gil had broke Rand's neck."

Ollie Ladd put his heavy glance on Jed Mims.

"That's poor talk. I don't like it."

"Well, now," retorted Jed, "mebbe I don't give a thin damn whether you do or not. No law against a man statin' an honest opinion."

Ollie Ladd began to bristle, growling deep in his throat. Jake Dolwig stopped him with sharp words.

"A minute, Ollie!" Dolwig, who had gone around behind the bar, now faced the hulking deputy levelly across it. "Do you bring anything legal to Yeager?"

"Legal!" blurted Ollie. "How do you mean, legal?"

"You got a warrant for him, maybe? You aiming to slap an arrest on him?"

"Well—no." Ollie floundered a little. "I'm just tellin' him—"

"You needn't!" snapped Dolwig bruskly. "You brought the news about Rand's jaw. That's enough. We can do without any extra bully-puss. Which makes this a good time, I think, for me to tell you something, Ollie. Any time you come into my place on strict official business, then I got to take your swagger and like it. But when it isn't official, then I don't have to take anything from you. Neither do my customers or my friends. Is that clear?"

Alert verbal repartee had never been a strong point with Ollie Ladd. His world was strictly physical, ruled by reliance on brute strength and imposing bulk. Now, made uncertain and uncomfortable by Jake Dolwig's flat pronouncement, he shifted and glowered, then went ponderously out.

Gil Yeager was still staring at his fist, flexing and unflexing it. A faintly somber shadow lay in his eyes. Jed Mims, observing, spoke quickly.

"Be glad it was his jaw, not yours. If it had happened the other way round, he wouldn't be caring the littlest damn bit. What you need is another drink."

Yeager shook his head. "What I need is to get out of town. Who you riding with now, Jed?"

"If you mean what outfit, not any. I been siwashing it back in the Coulee Glades with old Alec Trezevant and his girl."

Yeager dug some greenbacks from a pocket. "Starting now, it's you and me again, just like in the old days. We'll need grub and blankets and such. Go over to Patch Kelly's and order up what we'll want. I'll get a pack horse from Johnny Hock's corrals."

Jed Mims studied him for an intent moment. "I'd ask one question, boy. You still figger there's room for any kind of skim milk thinkin' on this prairie?"

"No, Jed," Yeager told him steadily. "Not any at all."

"Why then," said the old rider, reaching for the money, "I reckon we're a pair, you and me."

Crusty, blunt spoken, rawhide tough, Jed Mims tramped out of the Lodgepole, got his horse and led it across street to Patch Kelly's store. The Benedict buckboard was still drawn up there, with Laurie Benedict now on the seat. A sack of supplies was stacked in the back of the rig and as Jed Mims brought his horse up to the rail, Burke Benedict came out of the store with a second sack. He dumped this beside the other, untied his team and climbed to the seat beside his sister. He looked down at Jed Mims.

"How is he?"

"Huh?" grunted Jed. "Oh, you mean Gil? He's all right. He's fine. Can't say as much for Brick Rand, though. Word is, Gil broke Rand's jaw. Which," added Jed defiantly, "is all right, too. High time somebody got up nerve enough to bust something in that combine crowd."

Looking straight ahead, Burke gathered up the reins.

"Seen anything of Alec Trezevant lately, Jed?"

Jed ducked under the rail and pulled himself up on the porch before answering. Then he turned and considered Burke with eyes that were faintly hostile.

"I see him regular. Him and his girl, Anita, and me, we got a camp set up back in the Coulees. Which is all right for a pair of old leather-heads like Alec and me. But a girl like Anita, she deserves something better. She's the right to a decent roof over her head. Not that she's complaining any, understand. She'd never complain, Anita wouldn't. She's the pure quill, that girl!"

The line of Burke's jaw tightened a little.

"The Trezevants are welcome at the Benedict ranch at any time and for as long as they wish to stay. They know that."

"Mebbe," said Jed Mims with remorseless brevity. "But I guess they got their own reasons for preferring a camp in the Coulees."

Burke said nothing more. He kicked off the brake, spun

42

his team, and, using the whip, had them stretched out and running by the time they had gone ten yards. His jaw was set, the sweat of a caged anger lay across his cheeks, and his eyes were full of a stormy bitterness. Not until the buckboard hit the rutted roughness of the road beyond town and there started to careen and sway wildly, did he leave off using the whip and pull the team down, snorting and uneasy, to a milder pace.

"Damn them!" he gritted tightly, "damn them all! Who are they to rawhide me? What have they ever done to give them that right?"

Under the burn of renewed anger he again lifted the whip. Laurie caught his arm. For a moment he resisted. Then he relaxed and lowered the whip.

"Sorry," he said gruffly. "Stupid of me to take it out on the team. But if a man's any good at all, he needs the regard and respect of others like him. Else it's a tough chore to keep his head up and his back straight."

Laurie, nodding soberly, stared into the high prairie's sunlit distance.

"I know. Neither is it easy to be pleasant to someone you'd rather not be around."

Burke looked down at her quickly. "Has Meade Bastian stepped out of line?"

Laurie shook her head. "So far he's been the perfect gentleman."

Burke's big hands tightened about the reins. "He better be. The day he changes to something else, that day I break his damned neck. And to hell with the consequences!"

Between the moderate, timbered crests of the Redstone Hills and the loftier, darker bulk of the Seminole Mountains to the east, Summit Prairie ran its fifteen mile length. The upper ten of this lay in a virtually true north-south line, but the lower third, curving about the base of Sheridan Peak, angled east, following the down-running taper of the Seminoles into the Chinkapin country.

In the bight of the prairie's angle the town of Tuscarora stood, dominated by Sheridan Peak to the extent that for a short time in late fall and early spring, the sun in its seasonal swing was blocked by the mass of the peak, and its light and warmth relatively late in reaching town. At midsummer, however, the sun rose early to the north of the peak, and today, when Gil Yeager and Jed Mims rode out of Tuscarora with a packhorse at lead, it was blazing high and warm and clear.

Free of town, Yeager knew an uplift in spirit, a certain eagerness replacing the residue of harshness that had held him since the fight. Riding beside him, Jed Mims spoke without turning his head.

"It most generally takes two to stir up a ruckus. You didn't have to mix with Rand. With him havin' three others to back his hand, you could have held off and nobody would have blamed you. Instead, you tangled with him, so you must have wanted to. And I'm wonderin'—why? Because, if he had done a job of curryin' you, instead of the other way 'round—well—!"

Yeager shrugged and his words ran dry. "Last time I was on this prairie, Jed, I seem to have left the impression that I was afraid to fight. It was an idea I wanted to correct. And I couldn't think of a better time and place."

Jed threw him a quick glance.

"It ain't just being willin' to fight that counts so much as it is—how tough are you going to fight? You did all right against Brick Rand; you did fine. You made a damn good dog out of him. But you can't stop there, and if you figger to go all the way in this thing, then a little fist thumpin' rates as mild, even if you did bust his jaw. Speakin' short and to the point, Gil—how much are those guns for show, and how much for use?"

For some little distance Yeager kept silence, his eyes pinched down and fixed on the open sweep of country ahead. When he did speak his voice was low and even, but harsh, and his words full of bleak recollection.

"I spent a lot of bad nights when I was on the dodge, but there was one in particular, the wildest I ever knew or hope to know. I was crossing the Greystone Mountains, working out the trail of Shad Emmett. The storm hit just at dark. It threw everything at me. The thunder was like the world falling down. The dark turned so thick I couldn't see my hand in front of my face except when the lightning struck, which was plenty and often. Three different times it splintered trees only a few yards away from me. The air was full of the damn stuff. I could smell it, I could taste it.

"Then there was the wind. If you faced it square, you couldn't breathe. It ended up killing the horse I was riding, by blowing down a heavy limb which dropped right across the poor brute's neck, barely missing me. That put me afoot. It rained—you've no idea how it rained! I was half drowned, floundering around in a wild, black, half drowned world. Then the rain turned to sleet and my clothes froze on me. I couldn't find shelter and it was useless to try and light a fire in all that wind and water. The only way I kept from freezing to death was by moving, moving. Yeah, that was a night! I came through it alive, but I'll never know how."

Yeager's words dwindled out and he rode in silence while searching pockets for smoking. His glance was still fixed straight ahead and his lips were set to a tight and bitter line. Presently he went on, in that same bleak monotone.

"I kept remembering why I was out there, taking that kind of punishment. I kept remembering the way my horse went out from under me when that falling limb hit, and what could have happened to me if the horse had been just one small step further ahead. I thought of where, by rights, I might have been and should have been—back on Summit Prairie, warm and dry under my own roof. I thought of why I wasn't, and who was to blame. Yeah, Jed, I thought of so many, many things. And while that night was the worst one, there were a lot of other bad ones. So, if you think I came back here and bought a couple of guns just for the hell of it, you couldn't be more wrong!"

5.

FAR BACK IN the lavender-misted depths of the Seminoles to the north of Sheridan Peak, the clear, mountain-sweet waters of Aspen and Coulee Creeks joined, thence to storm white-foamed through the rocky length of Rubicon Canyon before emerging on the prairie flats as Rubicon Creek and move leisurely across these to empty into the silver glitter that was Heron Lake.

Just south of where Rubicon Creek left its canyon and where the first swell of the Seminoles began to lift from the prairie, the Benedict ranch headquarters crouched against a background of pine timber that spilled down from the higher slopes; a group of buildings whipped to a dun neutrality by years of sun and wind and weather, with corrals and fenced pastures reaching out along either side of the road so that the final stretch was a quarter-mile length of lane.

Rolling along this, the wheels of the buckboard and the chopping hoofs of the team stirred a slow-lifting funnel of dust. There had been little talk between Burke and Laurie Benedict since leaving town, and none at all since the ranch turn-off from the main north-south prairie road a good mile back. Both had drifted into the solitude of their own thoughts, and with each these thoughts had built a sober gravity.

Where the lane ended and the wide interval between ranchhouse and lesser buildings began, the buckboard crossed through the shallow water of a ditch which came down out of a narrow gulch off the mountain slope, ran its rough circle about the ranch headquarters, then angled north and west to join presently with Rubicon Creek.

As the splash of disturbed water and the good fragrance of its wetness came up to her, Laurie Benedict sighed, straightened, and put her glance on the white haired figure sitting in a big armchair at one end of the ranchhouse porch. The soberness of her expression did not break, but a swift gentleness shone in her eyes and softened her lips.

As Burke swung the buckboard to a stop at the ranch-house steps, Cam Reeves crossed over from the corrals. He gave Laurie a hand down, then tipped his head toward that white haired figure in the armchair.

"He hardly ever speaks any more, Laurie, but when he does it's always about you. This mornin', when I brought him outside, he asked for you, real anxious. Wanted to know where you were and when you'd be back." Cam paused, then added gruffly, "Seems like he just keeps shrinkin' up and gettin' further and further away from us all the time."

Cam moved to take care of the team while Burke unloaded the sacked supplies. Laurie went swiftly along the porch to the figure in the armchair, bent and swept her lips against a furrowed cheek.

"Uncle Dave," she murmured, "it's so good to be home with you again!"

The grizzled head tipped back and faded blue eyes looked up at her, eyes old and patient and gentle above a vague, small smile. He captured one of Laurie's hands and patted it. He did not speak.

As she went into the house, a swift twist of feeling tightened Laurie's throat. She thought, "It's like Cam Reeves said. Uncle Dave is moving further away from us all the time."

Burke, carrying the supplies inside, began stacking them on the kitchen table. Coming up beside him, Laurie said, a little fiercely, "I could hate myself for ever wavering even the slightest bit!"

Burke looked at her, silent for a little time while he considered both past and present. He nodded slowly.

"Here the same. He's never let us down for a second. So, we'll see things through as they are, Laurie. Whenever I begin feeling sorry for myself, then I remember the first time you and I ever laid eyes on Uncle Dave Benedict. Perhaps you don't recall things quite as clearly as I do, for you were only a little eight-year-old girl then, while I was a big thirteen. It was winter and we were in school when the word came, and I can still remember how the other kids looked at us, as if what had happened had suddenly made us different than the rest.

"A snow slide, we were told, had orphaned us, a slide that had buried our cabin home so deep that not until next late spring after the thaws had been well at work, would the cabin and what it held be visible again. Neighbors took care of us. The Archers—remember them? They were good to us and did the best they could, but somehow there was the feeling of not belonging. At that time the world and what it held ahead for me and my little sister was an awfully big and frightening prospect for a thirteen-year-old boy."

Burke paused, musing over those long past years and the scarring recollections they carried. He drew a deep breath.

"Then, one day, there came that kind and smiling man who was Dave Benedict, our uncle. Right away he filled the gap in our lives. He took us away from that mining town and brought us to this ranch. He anchored the world for us again, gave it stability, and once again we knew security and happiness. Now he's become an old man, and failing, and Doc Parris swears if he should have to leave the ranch he'd be dead within a week."

Again Burke paused, the line of his jaw taking on its characteristic stubborn squareness. He nodded, as though confirming a full considered and arrived at determination.

"So, we square our debt to him as best we can, Laurie—you and I. We smile and act pleasant with such as Meade

Bastian and Brick Rand, and so buy security from Summit Land and Cattle Company greed. We take the taunts and sneers of those who were once our good neighbors and friends, for playing what probably appears to them to be the part of peace-at-any-price laggards and cowards. All of which isn't at all easy for either of us. Yet, somewhere in the picture I feel we have just cause for some small portion of legitimate pride. Yes, we'll stick it, and an old and tired and muchly beloved man will know his last days in peace, on land that is literally his life."

While Burke spoke, a lump crawled up into Laurie's throat. She had to swallow hard to get rid of it. Huskily she murmured:

"You're right, Burke. We'll stick it."

Sighting past his horse's ears to the north, Gil Yeager kept steadily to the main prairie road. Way out ahead a haze of dust marked the progress of the Benedict buckboard. Watching this, Yeager saw it presently angle away from the main road and run on toward the misty notch in the flank of the Seminoles which was the mouth of Rubicon Canyon. Yeager recalled the many times in the old, good days when he had ridden that cut-off, and the pleasant world he'd found at the end of it; Laurie Benedict's world over which she had presided with so much warmth and charm. He wondered if ever again he'd find the same reward in the same world . . . ?

It was a thought which at this time and under present conditions made little sense, and he shook his head to be rid of it. The move made him swear softly, for it set up a renewed throbbing.

Jed Mims looked at him. "You cuss for the fun of it?"

Yeager showed a tight, mirthless smile. "I happened to shake my head. It was a mistake. For friend Rand hit me pretty hard, once."

"If you hadn't gone restless and stubborn so sudden," observed Jed, "we'd still be in the Lodgepole, restin' easy.

A few hours doin' just that wouldn't have hurt none. But no, you were all in a froth to get out of town. So now we're out, and if we're headin' for Alec Trezevant's camp in the Coulee Glades, we better start swingin' east pretty damn pronto, else when we do we'll have to cut plumb around the head of Rubicon Canyon, which ain't the shortest or easiest ride in the world."

"We'll end up in Coulee Glades all right," Yeager soothed. "But first, there's something I want to take a look at."

"What?"

Yeager was still for a moment before answering softly. "Home!"

"Was afraid of it," sighed Jed. "Boy, you won't like what you see. The combine has made it the main Sixty-six headquarters this side the lake. Likely enough, it's where Mitch Starker and them other two headed when Kline Hyatt run 'em out of town. You show there, you'll be lookin' right smack at trouble again."

"Trouble!" Yeager's eyes chilled and darkened as he brooded for a moment. "And Mitch Starker. He was the one who roweled me, wasn't he?" Reaching around, he slid a hand across the flat of his shoulder, and the contact set up a renewed smarting where the spur had dragged. "Yeah, Mister Mitch Starker. Now there is a fellow I want to meet again, Jed."

"He won't be alone," Jed warned.

Yeager swung his shoulders impatiently.

"Back in the Lodgepole you asked me if I felt there was room for any more skim milk thinking on this prairie. I told you there wasn't. It was that sort of thing which enabled the combine to grab all the acreage around the lake the way they did. Nobody wanted to take the first step toward a real fight with them. Including me."

He paused, considering this fact scowlingly.

"Maybe," he went on, "we just didn't believe they meant it until it was too late. Maybe we were all too damn selfish, figuring it would hit only the other fellow, in which case it wouldn't matter. However and whatever, one thing was certain. They had a fairly easy time of it because nobody stood up tall enough to really slug it out with them. Everybody seemed to take it for granted that the combine was just too damn big and tough to do any good against. But that was a year ago, and now it's today, and I'm wondering just how tough that outfit really is. Maybe it is high time we found out. Maybe today is a good time to start finding out. We'll see!"

Where Rubicon Creek met the lake, several acres of marshy meadow sprawled. The road crossed the creek just beyond the east edge of this, and when Gil Yeager left the road here he was riding on land that once was his. And still was, by God!

Abrupt acceptance of this fact brought him up high and solid in his saddle. He reined in and let his head swing and his glance run.

Off to his left beyond the ragged curve of the marsh, the lake waters began, now showing a faint rippling under the lazy push of a small breeze sifting in off the Seminoles. On scattered reed and tule clumps across the marsh area and along the lake borders, ruby-winged black birds clustered and teetered and dripped the clear, tinkling, silver rain of their song. Close at hand, almost from under the hoofs of his horse, a wisp of snipe fluttered up and zigzagged away, leaving their faintly rasping, "scaip-scaip" cry hanging in the air behind them. Somewhere in the marsh a mallard called, and far out over the lake a marsh hawk dipped and circled on alternately beating, then soaring wings.

This was an old picture to Gil Yeager, another of the many he'd hungered for during the past lonely, desperate year. Now he drank it in with the fervor of one renewed in many ways and dogged purpose rose in him. He squared himself in the saddle, his gaze fixed along the lazy-curving line of the lake shore to the north.

A short mile on, a ridge swooped down from the Seminoles, flowing into the prairie's flatness, losing height and bulk as it ran, so that by the time it reached the lake's edge it had shrunk to a low, rounded swell. Across this the road was a yellow-brown trace against the lighter tawniness of the prairie's sun-cured grasses. Beyond the swell of land that rose ahead was Yeager's immediate destination. He leaned in the saddle and stirred his mount to movement again.

They came up with cattle, all branded a crisp stampiron Sixty-six. Yeager, seeking some sign of his Lazy Y, found no evidence of it anywhere.

"What happened to my cattle, Jed? I owned some, once."

"Still do," Jed assured. "Most of that last herd you took into the mountains for summer range are still roamin' those wild brakes along the head of Aspen Crick. I'd have tried to bring that beef out if I'd had help and if there'd been any range to put it on. But there weren't no help and no open range, either. For by that time the combine had everything gobbled up. So the cattle had to winter in the mountains. Naturally there was some die-off, but most came through in good shape. I been ridin' that stretch of country regular to keep an eye on things."

"How many left, do you figure?"

Jed squinted thoughtfully. "At a rough guess, mebbe three hundred or a little better. Damn rough guess, though. You know how that country is. Man could throw a lot of cattle in there, give 'em a couple of weeks to scatter into the thickets and aspen swamps, then ride through casual like and swear up and down he didn't have half of 'em left."

"If we can save three hundred of that herd I'll be happy," Yeager said. "For only a little more than that went into the back mountains in the first place. But I also had close to two hundred head of yearling stuff on my lake meadows. What about them?"

Jed shrugged. "You guess."

"I will. And ask some damn pointed questions of certain people, too!"

They topped the swell of land and looked down at the headquarters beyond. Before the low, plain front of the ranchhouse a pair of poplar trees lifted, high and gracefully pillared in their mid-summer greenness. Between these stretched a hitchrail, and at this a saddle mount sagged, hip-shot and drowsing. Here also two men stood in argument of some sort, as one kept emphasizing his words by pounding a clenched fist into an open palm.

Over by the corrals, two others were busy, stripping saddles from three horses. Way out in a meadow along the lake border a rider jogged, and far distant up along the prairie road a thin lift of amber dust marked progress of some sort by someone.

Yeager raked the scene with quick, driving glances. This was the ranch home he'd last seen a year ago, and in no marked physical degree was it changed. Yet there was a difference, for here alien elements were present, felt as well as seen. Purpose, reckless and bitter, again rose in Yeager, thinning his lips, narrowing his eyes and sparking them with a cold fire.

"It's like I said it would be," Jed Mims reminded. "Starker and the other two did come here after Hyatt run 'em out of town. And there could be more combine hands around."

"No matter," said Yeager. "We're going in. Leave the pack-horse here."

He spurred down slope, Jed Mims at his heels, first swearing, then calling guardedly:

"One of those jiggers in front of the house is Mitch Starker. Other's the big boss of the combine—Meade Bastian!"

Alerted by the approach of Yeager and Jed Mims, the two Jed had named dropped their argument, turned and stood staring. Yeager drove right up to them, high and angular in the saddle.

"That's him," Mitch Starker said. "That's the one!"

So solidly and evenly built as to be physically deceptive, Meade Bastian was a bigger man than he seemed. His features were clean cut, a little on the narrow side; a handsome man but for two marring touches, one of which was a mouth

53

with a definite line of cruelty in it, the other a pair of eyes as blankly gray and merciless as those of a hunting hawk.

Gil Yeager recognized him as the one who had last night left Patch Kelly's store with Laurie Benedict. And meeting the impact of those strange eyes in which pupil and iris seemed to blend all to the same cold, unrevealing shade, he remembered something Johnny Hock had said.

"Yeah," Mitch Starker repeated, "that's Yeager. He half killed Rand with his fists. But if Brick had let me take him, it'd damn well been a different story!"

Meade Bastian considered Yeager with a long and unwinking intentness. Finally he spoke.

"The way you came down that slope, Mister, a man might think you intended doing something. If so—what?"

A cool one, Yeager thought. And sure of himself—very sure. Johnny Hock was right. This one was tougher stuff than Brick Rand.

"Well?" insisted Bastian.

Yeager made a small, swinging gesture. "Mine," he said bluntly. "All of it. Was a year ago, and still is. You got a week to clear out."

Meade Bastian stared. Then he put his head back and laughed. He was a smooth faced man, very brown, and his teeth glinted even and white.

"Mitch," he exclaimed, "we got a joker with us; good for a laugh even when he talks big. Yeah, Mitch—a joker!"

"Now there you're wrong," murmured Yeager. "It won't be funny—not funny at all, the way I'll handle matters. You heard what I said. A week to clear out. After that it could get rough. Oh, very rough!"

Bastian's laugh rang out again, then abruptly dissolved into a biting order.

"Because he made out mauling Rand, he's gone proud. He's a fool who needs a lesson. Mitch, yank him out of that saddle and give him one!"

While he spoke, Bastian was sliding a hand up inside the canvas coat he wore. Jed Mims' words hit him like a club.

"Don't try it, Bastian. Leave that shoulder gun where it is!"

Except for his head, Meade Bastian froze. But his head swung and he put his glance on Jed, who had drawn a gun and held it resting across his saddle horn, the muzzle tipped and looking down Bastian's throat. And now Jed gave further order in a harsh, warning yell.

"You two over at the corral—stay put and peaceful. Else it'll be too bad for Bastian. God damn it—I mean that! Stay put!"

Slowly Meade Bastian lowered his hands. His glance was blank and deadly.

"Friend," he said, his words carefully measured, "throwing that gun on me is the worst mistake you ever made. Your luck could fall apart before the week is out."

"And yours," was old Jed's harsh retort, "could run out right now." He put his next words at Yeager. "We aimin' to stay here all day?"

"Not quite," Yeager answered. "But somebody just said something that gives me an idea. Something about a lesson. And we got time enough for that."

With the words he spun his horse sharply. Mitch Starker, responding almost automatically to Bastian's order, had taken a couple of steps in Yeager's direction. Now, before he could guess Yeager's purpose and react to meet it, Yeager's horse smashed into him, and Yeager, leaning, grabbed at him.

Mitch Starker always wore a black and white calfskin vest, which was one of his dearest possessions. He treasured it because the color combination appealed to his somewhat aboriginal taste in such matters, and because in a visual illusory way it seemed to increase his size. Finally, he had also once heard it said that it made him stand out in a crowd.

Around the armholes and at the edges of the pockets the hair had worn thin, but the leather in the garment was still sound and tough. So it did not tear when Gil Yeager, reaching far, gathered in a solid handful of it between Starker's shoulders, hauled up hard, and set his horse to swinging in a fast, driving circle.

The move spun Mitch Starker completely off his feet, then dragged him around and around, cursing wildly as he tried to grab his gun and get his feet under him again. In neither attempt could he succeed, for the drag at his vest had pulled his arms high and trapped them so, while the increasingly fast swing of Yeager's horse was always ahead of his scrambling boots.

Holding his mount to that tight, spinning circle, Yeager now kicked his right foot free of the stirrup, hooked it over Starker's struggling figure and began swinging it back and forth and up and down. Mitch Starker's wild cursing broke off into a frantic bawl of pain. For the rowel of Yeager's spur ripped and tore, first at his shirt, then through this and into the flesh beneath, biting deep and bringing blood.

Around and around the tangle of men and horse whirled in a spurting haze of dust. Mitch Starker's yells of pain quickly thickened to a moaning hoarseness as the punishment from Yeager's spur, cutting and gouging, grew increasingly merciless. Starker's shirt ripped completely away, and his hairy torso showed torn and welted and smeared with welling crimson.

With a final swing and a last vicious digging rip of his spur, Yeager let go of his man, and Starker, rolling and sliding, slammed into the base of one of the poplar trees, his head snapping hard against this. He lay there, stunned, a half naked, bleeding hulk.

Yeager set his horse up, quieting it, while he put the heated bleakness of his glance on Meade Bastian.

"That's what I meant—when I said things—could—get rough." Panting breath from strenuous effort made his words uneven. He paused a little time before going on more steadily. "Maybe the next time that fellow Starker gets the urge to spur another man, he won't! All right, Jed—let's get out of here."

Jed wiggled the muzzle of his gun.

"You," he told Meade Bastian, "are taking a little walk. Jest in case one of them jiggers yonder by the corral gets ideas about a rifle and a try at some long range shootin'. Yeah, you're comin' along with us to the top of the rise. Get movin'!"

Bastian did not argue the point. He crossed the flat and climbed the low slope, with Yeager and Jed Mims riding along on either side of him. At the crest of the rise, Jed growled:

"This'll do. And about that luck business you mentioned—what d'you think of yours, now?"

Bastian did not answer. He merely put a grayly blank glance on either of them, then turned and strode back down the slope.

Jed Mims put his gun away, reached for his tobacco, let go a long sigh of relief.

"Am I glad that's over! What a pair of sittin' ducks you and me made, Gil, should a combine feller been hid out with a Winchester. Me, I felt as big and wide open as the side of Sheridan Peak."

Yeager spun up a cigarette of his own, shaking his head slowly. "Doubt they'd try anything as raw as that, Jed."

Jed snorted, slapped the heel of his hand against his saddle horn.

"Hell they wouldn't! Why d'you think I threw down on Bastian? Because he was reachin' for a gun, that's why. Listen, Gil, don't you make no mistake about that feller. He's bad stuff. He's the sort to kill a man just like he'd step on a bug if he figgered it'd gain him any profit."

"Maybe."

"Maybe—hell! I know he would. You ever see colder, queerer eyes in a man?"

"No," Yeager admitted, "I never did." He took a deep drag at his cigarette, then added briefly, "Your idea seems to be Johnny Hock's opinion, too."

"Damn right!" nodded Jed vigorously. "Johnny's smart." He peered at Yeager through a dribble of tobacco smoke, and now a hint of a smile pulled grimly at his lips. "Come to think of it, you weren't exactly gentle yourself, back there.

Goddlemighty, boy—I thought for a time you were fixin' to rip the innards right out of Mitch Starker. You sure cut him deep and plenty."

"Which I aimed to do," Yeager said. "Certain people should begin to get the idea, now." He leaned, caught up the lead rope of the staid old packhorse that had waited right where they left it. He straightened and put his glance on the misty rampart of the Seminoles. "We expect to hit Coulee Glades before dark, we better shuck along."

6.

BY THE TIME Meade Bastian got back to the headquarters, the others had helped Mitch Starker to his feet and over to the bunkhouse, where he now sprawled on a bunk. His eyes were dull from shock and full of a mixture of animal rage and pain and fear. Across his lower chest and naked belly and around one flank the flesh lay raw and quivering, smeared and caked with blood and dust. He looked up at Bastian and mumbled accusingly.

"Why didn't you stop him? Why didn't you do something?"

Bastian did not answer. His face was impassive, still, only the deep, cold glitter in his eyes giving true hint of his feelings. When he did speak it was to the other riders.

"Help him get cleaned up. I'll send Doc Parris out from town."

"No need," Starker blurted. "I ain't that bad off. And I don't want word of this spread around."

Bastian shrugged, turned to the door. "Suit yourself. You'll live, no doubt." He went to the horse tethered in the shade of the poplars, stepped into the saddle and reined away to the town road.

Back in the bunkhouse, his wits clearing, Mitch Starker refused any further aid. He rested for a time, then climbed up off the bunk. He still had on his calfskin vest, which, now pulled out of shape and stained with crimson, looked bizarre indeed over his naked torso. He shucked out of it and tossed it aside. Then he went out to the wash bench beside the bunkhouse door. Here was a tin basin, a bucket of tepid water and a none too clean towel that hung from a wall peg. With these he began washing the blood and dust from his punished body.

There was a lot of pain in him, a raw and smarting misery of the flesh as well as a pounding headache from his collision with the poplar tree. But these were as nothing compared to the dark and bitter revulsion of his thoughts.

What he had gone through, he brooded, was worse than any mere physical beating; far worse even than what had happened to Brick Rand, despite the fact that Rand had a broken jaw. For Rand had got it in an open, man-to-man fight, and with a thing of that sort, no matter how savage the final outcome, losing was never a lasting disgrace, providing a man did his best and put up as good a fight as he knew how. But this that had happened to him—Mitch Starker —was different.

He had been roweled, spurred to a raw and bloody mess, which was worse than any broken jaw. For a broken jaw would mend, while maybe a man never did recover from a spurring. Which did more than just punish a man physically. It was like using a horse whip on him. It demeaned him, put a stain on him, made him lose caste in the eyes of other men and knocked apart the foundation of his own self-respect. It could even gouge so deeply inside him as to reach where his spirit lived and so rob him permanently of much of his courage.

A groaning curse broke from Mitch Starker's lips, as if once again he was feeling the merciless rip and drag of Gil Yeager's spur. He shook himself and continued to curse, tonelessly and stupidly, while he dabbed water against his chest and belly and let it run down and gather wetly at the waist band of his jeans.

There was, he told himself, but one way he'd ever regain the things of the spirit which Gil Yeager's savage spur had torn out of him. He would get back all that he had lost on the day he saw Gil Yeager lying dead at his feet. . . .

Reaching town, Meade Bastian rode directly to the Golden Horn. Before dismounting he made full survey of the street, thus observing Ollie Ladd taking his ease on the courthouse porch. He caught Ollie's eye and waved a beckoning hand, and as Ollie came ponderously along, stepped down and tied.

"Where's Hyatt?"

"The office," Ollie said.

"Go get him. Tell him I'll be in Duke's back room."

Ollie nodded and went away. Bastian turned into the shadowed gloom of the saloon, where a lone bartender faced the room's emptiness and listlessly polished glasses.

"Duke?" Bastian asked, nodding toward a rear door.

"Yes," said the bartender.

Bastian moved along to the rear door, opened it and went through. Here was a square, fair sized room with a small safe in one corner, a table, and several chairs scattered about. In one of these, drawn up at the table, Duke Royale sat, a half burned cigar in his lips. He removed this and said:

"Been expecting you. Starker gave you the word about Rand?"

"He did. And now is in near as bad shape as Rand."

Duke Royale straightened in his chair, his hard, obsidian black glance suddenly intent. "What do you mean?"

"I mean the same one who worked Brick Rand over, rode in at the Rubicon Creek headquarters and spurred the tall hell out of Mitch Starker."

"This fellow Yeager was out there?"

"Him and that damned old wolf, Jed Mims. Yeager collared Starker and worked him over with a spur. I mean that, literally. He tore Starker's shirt off and cut his marks all up and down Starker's hide."

Duke Royale settled slowly back. "And you let him?"

"I let him. You would have, too. Don't—" here an edge of anger came into Meade Bastian's words and made them brittle, "don't try and throw the big pose at me, Duke. You never saw the day when your nerve reached any further than mine, or that you could lick me, for that matter. That little point's been settled a dozen times since we were kids. I let Yeager work Mitch Starker over because Jed Mims had a gun stuck down my gullet. Now you know!"

Bastian hooked a chair with his toe, dragged it closer and sat down.

"Yeager did more," he went on. "He gave us a week to get the hell off Rubicon Creek. Which was a laugh to me until I saw what he did to Starker. When you couple that with what he did to Brick Rand, why then you quit laughing and start thinking, hard!"

"Thinking—what?"

"That we got a tough one on our hands."

Duke Royale spun the tip of his cigar in his pursed lips, then removed it and let out a thin blue line of smoke.

"Tough man, maybe. But only one."

"Toughness can rub off on others," observed Bastian. "A tough leader can stir up tough followers. A lot of people on and around this prairie don't think much of the Summit Land & Cattle Company—of 'the combine'—as they call us. We'd be damn fools not to recognize that fact and realize what it might do to us, given certain conditions."

Duke Royale considered for a moment, then shrugged.

"Anything is possible, of course. But in this case I think you're borrowing trouble, Meade."

"Not borrowing it," retorted Bastian, "just figuring how to head it off."

"Sounds to me like Yeager's trying a long bluff," Duke Royale said.

"Ask Brick Rand and Mitch Starker about that. They'll tell you there's damn little bluff in a broken jaw or a hide

61

clawed raw with a spur rowel." Bastian shook his head. "No, Yeager wasn't bluffing. He meant every word he said."

Duke Royale smiled thinly. "Then you're suggesting we bow our heads and get off Rubicon Creek?"

Meade Bastian leaned forward and thumped a fist on the table.

"You know better than that. And wipe that damn smirk off your face! Just remember that while the black-eyed brother thinks he's the all-wise one of the two, the gray-eyed one feels just the other way about it. And—"

Duke Royale swung a warning palm, murmured swiftly:

"Easy, you hotheaded idiot—easy! Don't give the family history to the whole world. Somebody's out there!"

"Probably Kline Hyatt," Bastian said curtly. "I sent Ollie Ladd after him."

Footsteps echoed the length of the saloon, stopped beyond the door. Duke Royale called—"All right."

Kline Hyatt came in. He looked at Meade Bastian.

"Ollie said you wanted to see me."

Bastian nodded. "Pull up a chair. Duke, you got a couple more cigars?"

Duke Royale supplied the smokes. Bastian and Kline Hyatt lit up, Hyatt with a slow, guarded care. After which he sat quietly, his glance straight ahead, saying nothing, answering nothing. Meeting Bastian's eyes, Duke Royale gave just the faintest shrug, then settled back and also held silence. Bastian got to his feet and took a restless turn up and down the room. He came to a stop in front of Hyatt.

"That fellow Yeager was out at our Rubicon Creek headquarters today."

"Yes."

"Yes! He manhandled Mitch Starker. Used a spur on him. Tore him up pretty bad."

Kline Hyatt took his cigar from his lips, surveyed the tip of it. "That," he said meagerly, "is what Starker gets for trying to use a spur on Yeager, after Yeager finished with Rand."

"I saw no signs of such on Yeager," Bastian protested. "But Mitch, he's all ripped to hell."

"Then he should have learned a good lesson," Hyatt said, still frugal with words.

"Maybe you don't get what I mean," Bastian said. "I'm telling you that Yeager used Mitch Starker wicked. Wicked enough to be arrested for it."

"Thought you might be coming to that," Hyatt nodded. "Starker's not dead or dying, is he?"

"No. But—"

"Well, then," cut in Hyatt, "if you want Yeager arrested, you go before Judge Carmody, swear out a complaint and get the Judge to issue a warrant of arrest. You do that, I'll bring Yeager in. Otherwise I'm not interested."

Bastian swung sharply away across the room, his eyes beginning to flare.

"Sounds like a hell of a lot of useless rigamarole to me. Don't tell me you have to go through all that before you can step out and arrest a man?"

"In this case I do," Hyatt said.

"But why, damn it—why?"

"Because that's the way I operate now, strictly legal in every respect. And I warn you that you'd better have a thoroughly sound and justifiable charge to lay before Judge Carmody, something a lot more substantial than one based on the fact that a known bucko boy like Mitch Starker took a physical going over which he's long been asking for. Otherwise you'll probably bump into an official call-down you'll date time from."

Again Bastian stopped in front of Hyatt, lips pulled to a thin, hard line.

"Sounds almost like you might be going proud on us, Hyatt. Why a year ago—"

"Past history," Hyatt cut in. "A thoroughly venal man, Elias Blackmur, was sitting on the bench then. Today he stands discredited, suspended under Territorial Court order, waiting trial and prosecution for collusion and a lot of other things. Between him and a man like Judge Carmody, there is no slightest judicial resemblance."

"You went along with Blackmur," Bastian reminded.

Kline Hyatt shrugged. "I performed orders that came out of his court. That most of them would hardly stand the light of day was no fault of mine. But as I say, that is past history. And today the picture is different."

"How different?"

"Simply that there's a strictly honest court on this prairie now."

The tight line of Bastian's lips twisted. "It's like I figured. You're going proud and noble on us."

"No," said Hyatt. "Not proud or noble. I'm just being realistic. And perhaps making it a little easier to live with myself."

Duke Royale spoke, with a soft casualness which did not hide the pressure behind his question.

"When is the next election, Hyatt?"

Hyatt swung his head and looked at Royale through a long moment of inscrutable stillness.

"A year from now. Why?"

"You're wanting to be retired, maybe?" The tone was still casual, but the pressure and the threat had deepened.

"No," said Hyatt. "Not wanting to be, and I won't be."

Behind the casual manner Duke Royale presented outwardly, an inner impatience had been mounting. Now it broke into the open, and he threw contemptuous words at Kline Hyatt.

"You'll stay in office only so long as Meade and I want you in there. You'll wear that star only so long as you remember who your friends are—and act accordingly. The day you forget to do that, Hyatt, you'll be kicked out like any other damn dog that turns against a master!"

Turgid color darkened Kline Hyatt's face. As he stared at Royale, his eyes pinched down to mere slits. He rose slowly to his feet, and of a sudden was a far harder, tougher man than when he'd first entered this room. His voice ran flat—harsh.

"Royale, you just put your foot in your mouth. What you said decides things for me, makes up my mind. Now I've always believed in practical politics, and I've played those of my office right up to the hilt. Because I've been around long enough to know that sort of thing is more or less necessary if a man wants to hold on to his star—which I do. At the same time, while I've been willing to bend a little, this way or that as conditions or circumstances seemed to warrant, any man who tries taking a club to me, makes a mistake. And you just did, Royale. You just made a bad mistake!"

Hyatt stepped over to the door, then faced the pair of them again.

"From now on, if either of you want to see me, you'll come to me. Don't try sending for me, as you'll be wasting time. And, Royale—if you think you're the master and I'm the dog, here's the time for you to prove it. Go ahead, God damn you—let's see you kick me out!"

Neither Meade Bastian or Duke Royale moved. For here plainly was a man cocked and ready and full of a deadly danger. Kline Hyatt's lip curled.

"Just so! This proves who's the dog—and it's not me!"

Saying which, he went through the door and closed it soundly behind him.

Duke Royale stared across the room, his eyes all hard, wicked, black glitter. Trying for the solace of tobacco smoke, he found his cigar gone dead. With an explosive gesture he threw the butt aside and swung around to face Meade Bastian.

"Well," murmured Bastian sardonically, "what do you think now?"

Duke Royale did not answer while he set another cigar going, using this small segment of time to get his feelings under control again. He succeeded in this only partly, for when he spoke it was with a savage, convulsed anger.

"He's an arrogant fool, and needs a damn good lesson!"

Meade Bastian shook his head. "I'll go along with only part of that—the last part. Hyatt could stand some convincing, all right. But you were the arrogant one, not him. And he's no fool. Politic-wise, he's as shrewd as they come. He wouldn't be going stiff-legged on us unless he sees something shaping up which he figures could give us considerable trouble."

Royale made another abrupt gesture. "We got this prairie in our hip pocket."

Bastian puffed strongly on his cigar and his eyes were frowning and thoughtful as he squinted through the smoke.

"Maybe we have," he said slowly. "Yeah, maybe! And whether we can keep it so is something else again. It could be, you know, that we've grown fat and smug. Maybe things have come too easy for us. We took over this prairie with damn little trouble, when you stop to think of it. We moved fast, bluffed and faked, and pulled only a few really tough strings. Ranchers like Yeager and old man Trezevant— that Dutchman, Hans Ogaard and the rest, they were surprised and caught off balance. They never did have the chance to organize."

"There's no fight in that crowd," Royale stated. "If there was, they'd have shown some long before this."

"Maybe all they've needed was a leader," Bastian reminded. "And now they could have one."

"You mean this fellow Yeager?"

"I mean Yeager."

"There wasn't anything to him a year ago. In fact, from what Brick Rand reported then, Yeager was easier to handle than most of the rest."

"Which could have been because he had less chance to get rough than any of the others. Almost before he knew what was going on, he was behind bars. Besides," Bastian added drily, "as Kline Hyatt would remind us, that was a year ago. And Duke, did you ever stop to consider what we got to depend on in a real, all-out show-down?"

"We got what we've always had—the organization. And it's a good one, which we've come a long way with."

"A good one," Bastian said slowly. "Sometimes I wonder—how good? Certainly it can be no better than the men in it. And how good are they? Until today I'd have picked Brick Rand and Mitch Starker as two of the best and the toughest. But it turns out they weren't near tough enough. For this Gil Yeager, this easy mark of a year ago, has just plain whipped the tall hell out of both of them. If I've learned anything in the past twenty-four hours, it is that all men can change. As witness Kline Hyatt. No, Duke—it comes to me that perhaps we've been taking entirely too much for granted."

Duke Royale made a turn up and down the room, trailed by a banner of cigar smoke. When he finally paused and spoke, some of his assurance was gone and his tone ran thin and disturbed.

"Damn you and your logic! I don't like the sound of it. Yet I must admit that it is—logic. Where does it leave us?"

"Facing realities and acting on them."

"Go on," Royale said. "There's more to it than that."

"This time yesterday," Bastian said, "all was peace and quiet. Then, last evening some time, Yeager rides into town. From that moment, things have happened. Kline Hyatt, who was in our corral as late as yesterday, is now outside it and showing his teeth. Brick Rand, who was tough enough to get us our start here on Summit Prairie, is laid up in the hotel with a busted jaw, and maybe a busted nerve. Mister Yeager's work. Mitch Starker, another of our best bucko boys, is out at the Rubicon Creek headquarters, spurred raw. Yeager again. While I had cool ultimatum thrown in my teeth by this same fellow, Yeager. I say the man is dangerous—damn dangerous. I don't care what he was a year ago. Today he's trouble. And he could turn out the bee to set all the others buzzing."

They stood for a little time, facing each other across the round, green-felted table. Presently Duke Royale stirred.

"One answer comes to me."

"Yes?"

"The only permanent one."

"Yes?" said Bastian again, with rising inflection.

"It is simple enough," Duke Royale said. "Where there is no bee, there is no buzz."

Meade Bastian smiled, and in the pull of his lips an abrupt cruelty flared.

"Duke, you read my mind."

7.

DUSK WAS A blue-black tide flowing out of the Redstone Hills, to march across the prairie with giant strides and climb the serried flanks of the Seminoles, blotting out timbered slopes and benches, surging up and up until only the extreme crests held the fading remnants of day's light. On Sheridan Peak, cupped just beneath the rocky tip, an aspen thicket, early turning, gave out a last reflected gleam of the palest silver and gold. Then, abruptly, this too faded and darkened and the young night was absolute.

Through deep, chill dark, Gil Yeager and Jed Mims rode into one of the larger of the Coulee Glades. At the far end of this, tucked against an aspen grove, Alec Trezevant's campfire burned a ruby hole in the gloom. At sound of the approach, dim figures moved warily back into the shadows. Jed Mims sent his call ahead.

"It's all right, Alec—all right!"

As he and Jed Mims rode closer, the savory odors of cooking food reached Gil Yeager, reminding him of the fact that he'd had no food since early breakfast that morning, now a long twelve hours gone. And the intervening hours had been anything but mild and leisurely. Reined up at the edge of the fire-glow, he and Jed stepped from their saddles. In the further darkness there was a stir and a low exclamation of surprise.

"It's Yeager," somebody said. "Gil Yeager!"

The dim figures came out of the hiding darkness. A lank gaunt old man who was Alec Trezevant. A lank, gaunt younger one who was Harry Plume. And a stocky one who was Jack Swayze. Then a fourth figure who was slim and quick in a divided skirt and a man's woolen shirt, worn like a coat.

Yeager greeted the men with a reserved curtness.

"Alec—Harry—Jack!" But as he turned to the girl his tone gentled. "How are you, Anita?"

"Hello, Gil. It's good to see you again." The words were even and soft, the tone melodious. "You and Jed are just in time for supper."

Throughout a steadily lengthening interval, however, the three men of the camp said nothing, and Jed Mims, his glance swinging from one to the other, rapped out crisp words.

"Well, Alec—what is it? Do Gil and me stay here, or do we move on and make our own camp?"

Alec Trezevant cleared his throat harshly. "It'll do, here."

Maybe it would do, and then again, maybe it wouldn't, Gil Yeager mused while he unsaddled. It sure wouldn't if this present atmosphere endured. For Trezevant's welcome was grudging and with obvious reservations. Not on account of Jed Mims, of course. Jed was one of the old pack, accepted and believed in. He, Gil Yeager was the question mark.

A strained silence of suspended judgment held throughout the meal. But the food was plentiful and good, the substance and manner of the meal taking Yeager back to many similar ones. Venison, beans, dutch oven bread; coffee and a tart sauce of stewed wild plums. Finished, and reaching for his smoking, he tipped his head to the girl.

"Wonderful, Anita. I never ate better."

Her smile was quick, her dusky cheeks faintly touched with color. Her eyes and hair were dark, with high cheekbones giving a tapered outline to her face. There was eighth Blackfoot Indian blood in this girl, and it brought to her a warm, rich beauty. She began cleaning up the supper dishes and Jed Mims moved to help.

"Plenty bacon in that load of grub which Gil and me brought in, Anita," he said. "You won't run shy of fryin' grease for a while."

Over at the edge of the shadows where he sprawled, loose and gangling and uncouth, Harry Plume spoke in his thin, complaining way.

"Mebbe Anita ain't exactly anxious to cook for any army, Mims. Can't expect her to dish up grub for every stray that comes along."

Jed straightened and put his hard stare over there.

"And just what did you ever bring to this camp besides an empty belly and that damned 'poor me' whine you're always tradin' on? Should your conscience be really hurtin', Plume—which I sure doubt—then go eat your own grub or get over here and start swabbin' dishes!"

Harry Plume was a roan-headed man with a pointed, narrow face and grubby, dry cheeks; a calculating, penurious sort, forever ragged and unkempt. There was a skinflint's slyness in him, and a mean jealousy toward any other man who might win a smile or friendly word from Anita Trezevant. His eyes were small and muddy and they now burned angrily at Jed Mims. This same anger started pushing him to his feet, but Alec Trezevant waved him back.

"Let be, Harry. I said it was all right."

Alec Trezevant was a beaked, dark, bony old wolf, with skin like dressed saddle leather and coal black hair showing just the faintest touch of grizzle. His eyes were equally black and deep set under shaggy brows. Hunkered by the fire, arms folded across hunched knees, he sucked at a stubby pipe which snored and gurgled moistly.

Off to one side, while smoking out the last of a thin cigarette, Jack Swayze had been lounging on one elbow. Now he got to his feet and flipped his cigarette butt into the fire.

"I'll be shaking along, Alec. Obliged for the meal, Anita."
He would have moved off then into the dark, but paused at Yeager's call.

"A minute, if you will, Jack. I've something I'd like you to listen to."

Swayze hesitated, then turned and came back. He stood, stocky and solid, regarding Yeager through a short silence. He nodded curtly.

"Go ahead. I'm listening."

Yeager looked at Trezevant. "This for you, too, Alec. And for Gene Hickerson and Pete Blalock and Hans Ogaard, if they were here."

Neither Swayze or Trezevant said anything more. They merely waited, eyeing him without expression.

"There are," said Yeager quietly, "people who for some reason seem to feel it was mainly my fault the land and cattle combine was able to move in and take over on Summit Prairie. Just why that should be, I don't know, for I was only one among several with identical range and cattle interests around Heron Lake and across the prairie."

Harry Plume spoke up. "Yours and the Benedict layout were the only two on the east side of the lake. If you'd been willin' for the rest of us to move in with you, we mighta made a stand of it against the combine."

"How about the outfits on the west side of the lake?" Yeager retorted. "One of them yours. What happened there?"

"They hit us too quick. We didn't have time—"

"What time did I have?" cut in Yeager. "No more than anyone else. Your talk is hind sight, Plume."

Jack Swayze made an impatient gesture. "This all you wanted me to listen to, Yeager—you and Plume argue? If it is, I'll move along."

A stirring anger tightened the lines of Yeager's face, but he managed to hold his voice even.

"What I'm reaching for is some fair, open-minded thinking and the facing of a few facts. We on Summit Prairie were a pretty self-centered lot. When I say we—I mean all

71

of us. We'd done a lot of minor squabbling among ourselves over range boundaries, each of us quite willing to edge a neighbor out of a stray acre or two if we could. So, when the combine moved in, we were all too concerned with our own selfish little affairs to read the signs in the dust. Or, if we did, to care much, for some stupid reason apparently believing the lightning would strike only the other fellow."

"Now you're makin' sense," Jack Swayze said bruskly. "Keep on."

Alec Trezevant held silent, but slowly nodded. Harry Plume, however, came up with a grudging, sulky question.

"How was we to guess what the damned combine had in mind?"

"By the size of the herd they threw on the old Patrick range," Yeager told him curtly. "That should have made it plain that they intended to reach out and grab more grass. And that was when we should have got together and called for a showdown. But we didn't. And we're all at fault, equally."

Again Alec Trezevant nodded, while some of the bruskness leaked out of Jack Swayze.

"Admitting you're more than half right," he said, "ain't that some of the hind sight you just mentioned?"

"Yes," said Yeager frankly, "it is. Though I'm not using it with the idea of throwing the rawhide at anyone, but instead to clear up the picture, so we can start fighting back."

"Fighting back!" Swayze stared, quickening interest in his glance. "You figure it would do any good? That we'd have a chance, maybe?"

Grimly honest, Yeager shrugged. "I don't know. I aim to find out. If any of the rest of you are interested, I'll be glad to have you with me."

"Not me," exclaimed Harry Plume quickly. "As things stand I still got a few cows left, and I ain't aimin' to take part in anything that'll start the combine after me again and leave me with nothin' at all."

Yeager eyed him with open contempt. "That's all right, Harry. I wasn't counting on you, anyhow."

Harry Plume's dry cheeks pinched up and his tone shrilled. "Why should I go out on a limb for you? What did you ever do for me?"

"Why, nothing at all," Yeager said. "No, sir, Harry—not a thing. So we'll just leave you out of the picture." He turned to Jack Swayze. "You heading back for Chinkapin?"

Swayze nodded.

"You'll see Gene Hickerson, maybe? And Pete Blalock and Hans Ogaard?"

"Not Dutch Ogaard. He's left the country. Blalock and Hickerson I'll see."

"They satisfied the way things are with them?"

Jack Swayze let himself down on his heels beside the fire and began twisting up another cigarette. His answer came slowly thoughtful.

"Wouldn't know about that. What I mean is, I don't know whether they'd be of a mind to lay everything on the line in an all-out ruckus with the combine. But I do know that the way things stand now, Blalock and Hickerson and me, we're goin' broke, sure and certain. We've talked it over fifty times, I bet, tryin' to figger a way out. We ain't found any. So it could be that Gene and Pete would be willin' to throw in with you."

"And you, Jack?"

Swayze fixed a narrowed glance on the heart of the fire, dragging deep on his cigarette and letting a film of pale blue smoke filter from his lips.

"Now there's a thing a man's got to think on. For certain there ain't enough grass along Chinkapin to keep on grazing the number of cows Hickerson and Blalock and me got between us. Last winter we got by pretty good. This one, what with the cattle weakened down the way they are, there's bound to be a heavy winter kill. For us, there's only one answer, which is more and better range. But where to find it? Should we try and drive completely out of this part of the country, God knows how far and where we'd have to go before findin' some more free grass. Which sure is the only kind we could afford."

Swayze picked up a twig of pine wood, broke it into small fragments, tossed these into the fire.

"Hereabouts," he went on, a deeply troubled man slowly voicing his troubled thoughts, "the good grass is on the prairie, around the lake where we were before. Yet to get back there means an all-out fight, and a pretty damn desperate one against big odds. And a man would be a fool if he stepped into something like that without some kind of plan. Maybe you got one?" Swayze's glance lifted and touched Yeager.

Yeager nodded. "First move would be to get a foothold again on this side the lake."

"Where would that be?"

"My old Lazy Y headquarters."

Harry Plume laughed scoffingly. "With the combine sittin' on it, fat and secure? Hell of a chance you'd have, Yeager."

Silent up to now, Alec Trezevant swung his head, let out a rumbling growl.

"Shut up, Plume! You said you wanted no part of this, so stay out of it." To Yeager he said, "You got a plan. Let's hear the rest of it."

After considering a moment, Yeager spoke slowly.

"Except for the old Patrick range, the combine doesn't legally own a single acre of Summit Prairie grass. They're holding it purely on the basis of the old argument that possession constitutes nine points of the law. Actually, they're sitting illegally on range that is rightly ours. How to get them off? There are two ways. One would be taking our claims to court. But while we've an honest man in Judge Carmody now on the bench, we'd be faced with litigation we couldn't afford to pay for; the combine has money to drag that sort of thing on for God knows how long. Well, what move is left to us?

"Just one. That we use the possession idea ourselves. We

move in, quick and quiet, grab a chunk of range and sit tight. That leaves the next move up to the combine. They don't dare take their claim to an honest court because they have no legal leg to stand on, so they could get no court order to move us off. The only way they can move us is by force. They do that, they're outside the law, because we'll be defending land legally our own. If we get together on a deal like that—and stick together, we can make it mighty rough for them."

"Providin' the court ain't on their side," Jack Swayze argued. "It was before. Why won't it be now?"

"Because," explained Yeager patiently, "Elias Blackmur was crooked. Judge Carmody is an honest man."

"Kline Hyatt was the combine's man," persisted Swayze. "And still is, I'll bet."

"Maybe, maybe not," Yeager said. "Before, he was taking orders from a crooked court. Now he's got to answer to an honest one. That could make a big difference."

"Looking past all the legal this and that," Alec Trezevant said grimly, "unless either us or the combine backs down complete, chances are good things could end up in a smoke-rolling. Right?"

Yeager agreed. "That's right. And it's up to each of us to decide whether we want to face such."

"You figure to?" Alec Trezevant's black eyed glance dug deep into Yeager.

"Yes."

"Which," charged the old fellow, relentlessly harsh, "don't shape up like the kind of man you used to be."

Yeager said something he'd said to others. "A man can change, Alec."

"When I side a man," growled Trezevant, "I want to know he's going to stick."

"I'll stick."

Silent since setting Harry Plume down with cutting remark, Jed Mims now spoke up again.

"A couple of things you should know about, Alec. This morning in town, Brick Rand absorbed the lickin' of his life. Later, out at the old Lazy Y, Mitch Starker got spurred raw and Meade Bastian was told off, good! Gil did all those things. Mebbe such will help answer your questions."

Trezevant, his intent glance still on Yeager, stirred and brightened. His tone ran milder.

"Some marks on your face like you'd been hit. I was wondering about them. So you manhandled Rand, eh?"

"Some," Yeager said briefly.

"Some!" exclaimed Jed Mims. "Boy, you know better than that. I never saw a man worse whipped."

The harsh lines of Alec Trezevant's face relaxed into the ghost of a smile.

"I'd like to have seen that—I surely would. Brick Rand, he always figured himself a bucko boy, real mean and hostile."

"He's turned some fat and soft," Yeager said.

"What's this about Mitch Starker being spurred?"

Yeager shrugged. "When I finished with Rand, I was well whipped down, myself. Starker rode in close and tried to use a spur on me, which he'd probably have managed if Jed hadn't stepped into things just then. It's not an idea I like, being spurred. So, when I had the chance later on, I gave him some of his own medicine."

Alec Trezevant dropped his glance to the fire, the musing half smile still on his lips. He nodded his head slowly up and down, as though visualizing something he liked and approved of. He sucked at his pipe, found it dead, leaned forward and knocked the dottle from it against a piece of wood.

"You get ready to move back on your place," he said, "I'll ride with you."

Yeager drew a deep breath. This was what he'd hoped for, not only because Alec Trezevant, old as he was, would be wicked in a fight, but because his move could influence others.

"I'll be happy to have you along, Alec." Yeager turned to Swayze. "How about you, Jack?"

Swayze pushed to his feet. "I'll talk it over with Hickerson and Blalock and let you know tomorrow."

He moved off into the dark and soon the soft mutter of hoofs laid a diminishing echo through the night.

Harry Plume, lank and loose and sulky, moved over to where Anita Trezevant, finished with her dishwashing chore, had settled down cross-legged on a blanket back at the edge of the firelight.

She was a grave, still girl, who, thought Yeager as he watched her, lent a welcome note of grace and charm to this wilderness camp. Yet, unobtrusive and retiring as she seemed, there was spirit and fire in her, as Harry Plume now found out. Voicing some low toned remark, he would have dropped down beside her, but she repelled him with a quick, curt retort which straightened him up again and sent a flush of anger through his dry cheeks.

For a moment he stood hesitant, as though searching out words for reply. Before he could find them, Alec Trezevant's deep growl hit at him.

"You don't seem to be agreeing with anybody, Harry. You better drift."

Harry Plume made a hard, slashing gesture with the edge of his hand, whirled off into the gloom at a forward-leaning, lunging stride. Then again the ripple of hoofs diminished into the night, these at a run.

"Now there," observed Jed Mims drily, "rides a man plumb out of patience with the rest of the world. He keeps pushin' on the reins that way he's liable to run into a limb in the dark and knock his teeth loose."

"Any man," gruffly remarked Alec Trezevant, "has a right to use caution in his own affairs, so long as he ain't always playing both ends against the middle. He does that, then I can get damn impatient with him." The old fellow turned again to Yeager. "Seeing we'll be riding together, mebbe we better start some exact figgering on how we're to get back on your old headquarters stand. Daughter, stir up another pot of coffee!"

With a new day's sunlight beginning to spill down across the crest of the Seminoles, Meade Bastian rode up the lane between the fenced pastures of the Benedict ranch and crossed the ditch at the lower edge of the headquarters interval. The splash of water and the click of hoofs on gravel, brought Cam Reeves past the corner of a feed shed.

Meade Bastian nodded crisply. "Hello, Reeves."

A simple, honest man, Cam gave no reply, just stood and stared at Bastian, open dislike plain on his blunt, square features.

In Meade Bastian, besides an inherent streak of cruelty, there lay the strong ego of a virile, handsome male. This, together with the conceit of power, bred a pressing arrogance which could not stand to be ignored. He struck at Cam with thin, slashing tones.

"What the hell's the matter with you—you gone dumb? Were you riding for me I'd damn quick teach you some manners!"

Cam Reeves looked him up and down again, spat, turned and went off about his morning chores.

Bastian, quick rage flaring in his eyes, rowelled his horse savagely, and when the stung and startled animal would have surged into a run, hauled it back on its haunches with a heavy sawing of the reins. Trembling, snorting, the punished, bewildered mount sidled over toward the ranchhouse, head tossing.

Burke Benedict stepped out on the ranchhouse porch. He'd watched Meade Bastian's approach, observed the short byplay between him and Cam Reeves, and, knowing both men, pretty well understood what had taken place. He stood now in morning's sunlight, a towering, raw-boned, somehow brooding figure.

"Morning, Meade," he greeted. "Just about second coffee time. Light and have some with me."

Still seething, Bastian did not answer for a moment. Then he nodded and stepped from his saddle.

"I'll go you on that."

He dropped his reins and his horse swung away a little distance before reacting to the authority of the grounded, dragging leather. Even then it worked back and forth uneasily, still edgy and upset from the spurring. Sweat, starting suddenly, darkened its neck and chest.

There had been another spectator to it all. From a window of her kitchen, Laurie Benedict missed none of it, and the reaction clouded her eyes and put indignant color in her cheeks. When Meade Bastian and her brother Burke entered the kitchen, the cast of her head and shoulders was stiff and antagonistic. Quick to note this and guess why, Bastian forced a short laugh.

"I'm sorry, Laurie. But that rider of yours, Reeves—I give him decent greeting and he doesn't answer, just stares like a wooden Indian. I don't like that kind of treatment; it gets under my skin."

"I don't know anything about that," said Laurie curtly. "But I do know your horse was no way at fault. And I simply can't stand to see a helpless, dumb animal mistreated!"

Bastian shrugged. "Brute feelings don't reach very deep. If they did, think of all the misery we hand out when we brand and ear-mark a jag of cattle."

"In that there is necessity and reason," Laurie retorted. "Not senseless, needless abuse."

Meade Bastian's lips tightened. As long as he had known this girl she had never flayed him like this. His simmering feelings began to moil again.

"All right," he said shortly. "I stand corrected."

Burke Benedict moved into the breach. "Coffee, Sis," he said.

Laurie poured it for the two men, then, filling a cup

79

for herself, moved over to the window and stood looking out, the slanting sunlight glinting on her hair, building a glowing nimbus about her head. Over the rim of his cup, Meade Bastian watched her with narrowed, hard-surfaced eyes.

Months ago he had first seen and met Laurie Benedict and she had never ceased to attract him. For there was a fineness in her, an integrity beyond mere physical beauty which had challenged him, yet at the same time and for some strange reason, abashed the ruthlessness in him. Here was a girl he simply had to fully respect.

Until this moment, this day, she had never been anything other than quietly friendly. He had visited with her a number of times, had on a couple of occasions taken her to dances which the women folk of Tuscarora put on in the loft of Patch Kelly's warehouse. She had danced with him, smiled at him, laughed with him and ridden home with him through late night's starlight. Yet, in a deeply frustrating way, she had never been any closer to him than a million miles away.

It was a thing he couldn't figure, which puzzled, and to a degree, irritated him. For it cut at the man's conceit and his arrogance. Even so, until this moment, it had humored him to treat her with marked consideration and courtesy. This morning, however, she had for the first time shown him the real quality of her temper and had hit at him in open anger. And fire struck fire. He turned to Burke Benedict, his manner and words curt and chill.

"Your uncle Dave—how's he doing these days?"

Burke rolled a mouthful of coffee across his tongue before answering. "Fair," he said guardedly. "Times we think he's better, times not so good."

Bastian drained his cup, put it on the table and began spinning up a cigarette.

"He'll be with you a long time probably, providing he stays quiet and easy on this ranch. Be rough on him though, if you had to move him off."

Little knots of muscle bunched at the angle of Burke's jaw. "We never expect to move him off."

"Never," Bastian said, "is a long time. No man can figure that far ahead. By the way, what's your feeling about this fellow, Yeager? You satisfied to have him come back on the prairie?"

Burke shrugged. "I'd say that was his business entirely. They tell me he's been completely cleared of that Cress Lucas shooting charge."

"And they tell me," rapped Bastian bruskly, "that this Judge Carmody is a damned old fool who'll believe any fairy story if it's dished up to him slick enough. So just a hell of a lot of us aren't convinced that Yeager isn't a killer. We don't want his kind on this prairie and we're going to run him off it. Should he show here, send him packing. For he's just the sort to bring trouble to anybody who gets friendly with him."

Well, here it was again. Pressure and threat, partly veiled, partly open. Bow to the decrees of the combine or take the consequences. In an effort to keep the hoarseness of anger from his voice, Burke cleared his throat harshly.

"No reason for Yeager to show here."

"About that, you can't tell," Bastian said. "You never know." He took a deep drag on his cigarette, moved to leave. "Just dropped by to give you the word."

Sure, thought Burke savagely. That's all. Just came by to give the word. To show the clenched fist, you mean! May God damn you and all your kind, Bastian! And one of these days . . . !

At the kitchen door, Meade Bastian paused and looked at Laurie. Her back was to him still, her slender shoulders erect and defiant. Lips twisting, he hit out sardonically.

"Obliged for the coffee. But not for the welcome, Laurie. It wasn't worth thanks."

Laurie neither moved or answered. Bastian tramped out, with Burke following. Bastian crossed to his horse, gathered up the trailing reins and stepped into the saddle. From here he stared down at Burke and spoke some final curt words.

"Remember what I said. No help or comfort of any kind for this fellow Yeager!"

Burke drew a great, deep breath. "That's making it definite enough. You don't leave a man much choice, do you?"

8.

THEY CAME DOWN out of the Seminoles past the south rim of Rubicon Canyon and at the edge of the timber hauled up to test the night. Below them the prairie was an inky gulf, unbroken except for a single glitter of light far to the south where Tuscarora town crouched under the burly mass of Sheridan Peak. The stars were fugitive, their radiance smothered and held to the thinnest kind of substance by the late and heavy dark. From earth's deep stained blackness there was no responding reflection, but out where the waters of Heron Lake spread, a hint of translucent glow lifted, so faint as to be more illusory than real.

"Should be a good night for hell-raisin'," observed Jed Mims. "Time like this, you wake a man with the muzzle of a gun under his nose, he should gentle down fast."

Came Alec Trezevant's harsh comment. "Let's hope so. For there should be six of us in on this thing instead of three. Damned if I can get over that Chinkapin bunch. I never would expect any show of real nerve out of Harry Plume, but I did think better of men like Hickerson and Blalock and Swayze."

Gil Yeager eased himself in his saddle, slouching his weight in his off stirrup. "You can't blame them for being cautious and cynical, Alec. They've taken a lot of kicking around by the combine, and enough of that sort of thing can knock all the spirit out of a man."

"It can also make him damn good and mad," Trezevant growled. "Look at us. We took just as heavy a clubbing, maybe worse. And we aim to try and do something about it. But not them! Hell, no! Far as they're concerned they're apparently willing to just lay back and let everything go bust. And I can't figure any man doing that. When I been through a ruckus, even if I've absorbed a damn good licking, I still don't want all the pieces of hide scattered around to be chunks just off me."

"Nothing wrong with that gospel, Alec," Jed Mims said, "and I go along with you on it. But you know, the way Jack Swayze talked at first, I thought sure we could count on him. He must have figured that without Blalock and Hickerson, he better not come along."

"If that was his thought, I don't like it, either," Trezevant stated bluntly. "Damn a man who can't make up his own mind on a matter of principle!"

"Well then," murmured Jed Mims, "while we're layin' it on the line about who is and who ain't, what about Burke Benedict? He sure ain't actin' the part of any roaring lion. What's his idea, playing along with the combine, cheek by jowl? I always figgered you and Anita being pretty fond of Burke, Alec."

"That's right, we were," admitted Alec Trezevant slowly. "Time was when I rated Burke a lot of man, and I was happy to see him and my girl, Anita, hit it off so well. But now—I dunno." He shook his head.

"I can't figure Burke's stand any better than anyone else," said Yeager. "For that matter, we got no right to cuss out any man just because his point of view don't agree with ours. Maybe Burke's got the best reason in the world for playing his cards the way he does. But don't ever think that just because he ain't out there stomping and pawing up the dust that he lacks nerve. He's one of the quiet, easy-going kind that don't take fire too easy. But when they do—look out! They can be hell on wheels."

"My girl Anita has an idea about the Benedicts," Alec Trezevant offered. "She's worked it out from a couple of things Burke told her before her and him busted up over the damned combine argument. Anita thinks the reason Burke plays it friendly with the combine people is because of old Uncle Dave Benedict, who's a plenty sick man, and has been for a long time. Anita figures it's Burke's feeling that should the Benedicts ever get booted off their land by the combine, it'd probably mean a quick finish for old Dave. And if Anita's right in this," Trezevant ended gruffly, "it means that Burke's not only got nerve, but plenty of it. For it takes a lot more to stand up to a deal like that and hold in, than it does to blow and start swinging."

Gil Yeager straightened in his saddle, staring down through the night to where the Benedict headquarters lay formless and invisible in the dark. Here was an angle which, for some obscure reason, had not occurred to him before. And as he considered it now, it fitted and made sense. It could also account, he decided, not only for Burke's attitude, but for Laurie Benedict's seeming friendliness toward that fellow, Meade Bastian. Such a swift surge of satisfaction followed on the heels of this reasoning, it startled him.

If it's true, he thought, I sure got some apologies to make. . . .

He lifted the reins, set his horse to movement.

"Let's get along. This night isn't going to last forever, and we don't know just how much of it we'll need."

They dropped on down slope and the prairie lifted from the formless dark and let them on to its comparative level. They cut south of the Benedict headquarters, struck the main road and paused there to test the night again before heading north to cross Rubicon Creek and breast the low lift of land beyond.

Here the presence of the lake struck in strongly from the west, its moist, chill breath fanning their cheeks and the wet pungency of its shoreline flavors thickening the air about them. At the nearest marsh edge plover lifted and winged away, their startled crying coming back in a thin splinter of plaintive sound, while a distant coyote, foraging the lake's far margins, wailed its faint loneliness at the uncaring stars. Once there was a rush and the pound of hooves as a small bunch of disturbed cattle swung around behind them and raced back toward Rubicon Creek.

"A break," Jed Mims said softly. "Had those critters spooked straight away instead of circlin', somebody out yonder might have heard and wondered."

Atop the rise, Gil Yeager pulled up again. Ahead the objective of the night lay thick-shrouded by the dark, but in his mind's eye many details of the place were starkly clear. This thing he and Jed Mims and Alec Trezevant contemplated, could be relatively easy, or it could turn into disaster. It was something that had to be approached carefully and it would take both the element of surprise and a degree of luck to make it good. He stepped from his saddle, took off his spurs and hung them on his saddle horn.

"You two," he said, "stay put until you get my signal. From here you're in clear line with the cookshack door. If everything goes right, I'll flash a light twice at that door. In which case you'll come on in. But if I don't show any signal and I'm not back here inside half an hour, you head for Coulee Glades and forget all about me."

"If you're not back in half an hour, or if you don't show that signal," Jed Mims said tersely, "I'm comin' in lookin' for you."

Yeager turned to his horse, reached for his spurs again. "If that's the way you feel, Jed, we'll ride right out of here and to hell with everything. It's got to be the way we agreed on before we left camp, or not at all."

"All right—all right," grumbled Jed. "Have it your own damn pig-headed way. Just the same, two of us goin' in together would have a better all-around chance."

"Not if they got guards out," Yeager retorted.

He moved away afoot and began his stalk on the ranch headquarters. Just the faintest thread of night wind sifted down from the Seminoles, and Yeager circled to come in on his objective from the west, not only because by working into the drift of air small sound of his own approach would be muffled, but if guards were out, it would enable him to locate them and·their exact positions more easily. For men waiting out the long, lonely hours at such a chore would be sure to seek the comfort of tobacco, and the scent of cigarette smoke would drift far and close to the earth in the moist heaviness of the night air.

Actually, Yeager held strong doubt of any guards being set. The possibility that he and Jed and Trezevant would attempt so bold a foray as this would, in all probability, never occur to the combine heads. For the combine was big and the combine was powerful and fat with the carelessness of its own strength. Yet, with so much at stake a man would be a fool if he didn't make sure.

He came up to the west end of the ranchhouse without incident. He circled this cautiously, all senses straining for some sign of occupancy. Satisfied that there was none, he moved a shadowy, careful way about the rest of the premises, circling corrals and feed sheds, still looking for that not too probable guard. Finally convinced on this point, he became more direct and swift moving in his purpose.

He drifted past the bunkhouse and knew that here indeed were sleeping men. For the time he left them so, moving on to the cookshack. Through the open window at the rear end of this sounded the nasal drag and stutter of a man's snoring. Yeager smiled bleakly in the darkness. Ranch cooks, apparently, were all much alike; they liked to sleep close to their pots and pans.

He circled to the door, eased his way inside. Here ahead lay a ticklish part of this night's work. Any sort of alarm which would awaken men and set them on the alert could spoil everything; a single startled yell would do the business.

A year ago he could have moved through this building

and its contents with full assurance in any kind of dark, for then he was familiar with every inch of it. Now he must literally feel his way, inch by inch.

By its late lingering warmth he located the big cook stove at the rear of the room. To the left of this opened the door to the cook's sleeping quarters and presently Yeager stood in this, the sweat of tension a smarting moisture across his cheeks and along the back of his hands and wrists.

The cook still slept, but now more than the sound of snoring told of his presence. For here in this small room lay the acrid breath of a thousand ghosts of dead cigarettes, the mustiness of blankets too long used without sufficient airing, and all the other odors peculiar to close human confinement.

Yeager drew his gun. As Jed Mims had said, nothing slacked a man down more definitely when stirred to wakefulness during the small, cold hours, than the steel snout of a gun against his teeth.

Yeager edged his way toward the sleeper, gun held waist high, free hand extended, exploring for unseen obstacles. Somewhere in the Stygian dark of the room a clock ticked. Yeager's searching touch met the back of a chair and he lifted the chair noiselessly and set it aside. He located a small table, circled it and came up against the foot of the bunk. Moving along another careful step he found a second chair barring his way. This also, he made to shift to one side. In the move he tilted it slightly. Then came the faint scrape of metal on wood and with a jangling clatter an alarm clock slid off the chair and bounced on the floor.

In the straining silence the racket of this was like a cannon shot. The sound of snoring broke off in a strangled grunt, followed by a mumbled curse. Yeager flung the offending chair aside, reached and swung the heavy barrel of his gun in a short, chopping arc, hoping fervently that his guess at location was good.

It was close, but not quite good enough. Instead of clipping the cook across the head as intended, the clubbing gun barrel skidded down the side of his neck and spent its impact on the cushion of muscle at the angle of neck and shoulder. A numbing blow, but not a disabling one.

The cook's first mumbled curse became a stream of them carrying not only surprise, but pain and a desperate anger, and it was a fighting tangle of man and blankets that came whirling off the bunk.

This fellow was a thick and short and round man, with enough weight to him to drive Yeager against the table, which careened across the narrow room into the far wall with a rending crash. Yeager charged back desperately, reaching and grabbing. Fighting to get free of his blankets, the cook fell against Yeager, whose reaching left arm came down across the back of a heavy neck. Instantly, Yeager crooked his arm, hugging the man's head tightly, muffling the stream of gusty mouthings.

Whirling, the cook tried to shake Yeager off. But the blankets, low slipped now, tripped him and he went down, taking Yeager with him. Falling blind through the dark, Yeager's head clipped the side of the bunk and for a moment his world was full of spinning lights and numbing shock. He lost hold of his gun, but managed to hang on to his man, and, now setting the power of his right hand against his left, used both arms to tighten and maintain his clamping grip.

They rolled about on the floor. The cook's arms and fists flailed against Yeager's flank and across his back and kidneys, but he was unable to get enough purchase behind the blows to make them really effective. So now the fight began leaking out of him and fear emerged. He tried to yell for help. Yeager, sensing the up-coming effort, slid his arm still further about his victim's neck and across his nose and mouth.

Fighting only for precious air now, the cook began to struggle more and more frantically. In him was a man's mad urgency to breathe and live. His trapped breath piled up in his tortured throat in a strangled wheezing. Under Yeager's rigid forearm the pulse in his jugular was a violent throbbing.

Yeager had no desire to really harm this man. The initial

plan had been merely to locate a sleeper, awaken him under the threat of a probing gun muzzle and so hold him quiet. But the dark, a chair that stood in the way, and an alarm clock falling to the floor, had thwarted this. So now Yeager had no choice. And it wasn't a pleasant thing, strangling into insensibility a man against whom you felt no animosity.

The cook's desperate efforts peaked up, then swiftly dwindled. Yeager, slacking the pressure of his arms, knew deep relief at the harsh renewal of the cook's breathing. By the light of a match he reclaimed his gun. By the light of another he located a lantern hanging to a wall peg, and this he set aglow. He rolled the cook's limp figure over to the bunk and lifted him on to it.

Now Yeager carried the lantern to the main door of the cookshack. Here, after testing the blackness of the night and finding it still, he twice arced the light back and forth across the open door. After which he returned to keep an eye on the cook. This worthy, beginning to stir, coughed raggedly a number of times, then lifted his hands to feel of his throat. He pushed up on an elbow, blinking hazily at the gun muzzle being waggled under his nose.

"Sorry to have to treat you so, friend," Yeager murmured. "But it was a case of have to. Don't make me start in again. Just you keep quiet in all ways."

This suited the cook. He dropped back on his bunk and closed his eyes, a sick and considerably used up man.

Where it lay, the abused alarm clock still ticked loudly. Yeager recovered it and set it on the table, which, despite violent contact with the far wall, had remained upright. Yeager made a swift survey of the room for weapons, and found none. He was still at this when soft sounds at the door of the cookshack told of the arrival of Jed Mims and Alec Trezevant. Yeager showed them the light of the lantern to guide them into the back room.

"You cut the time kinda fine," grumbled Jed Mims. "We were beginnin' to worry."

Yeager shrugged. "Things I had to take care of. One was the cook. Meet him."

From the bunk the cook was eyeing these two new arrivals, his glance full of open alarm. He blurted a question.

"Mind tellin' me just what the hell's goin' on here?"

"Not at all," Yeager said. "The rightful owner of this property is reclaiming it. How many men in the bunkhouse?"

The cook blinked, shrugged. "Four. Mitch Starker and three others. What you aim to do with them?"

"Wake them up and send them packing. And we're going to tie you up, just to be sure you'll stay nice and quiet."

"That ain't necessary," the cook remonstrated. "I'm a pot wrangler. I leave fightin' to other people."

"Not entirely," Yeager said drily, feeling of his head where it had slammed into the side of the bunk. "I still think it wise to tie you up."

"Go ahead," mumbled the cook resignedly. "But I'm tellin' you I want no trouble."

Alec Trezevant produced rawhide thongs and secured the cook. "You yell," he growled, "I'll come back here and quiet you—plenty!"

"I ain't yellin'," the cook protested. "I ain't doin' a damn thing."

"Fine!" said Trezevant. "You're the smartest cook I ever run across."

Yeager carried the lantern and led the way to the bunkhouse. Here men still slept. They slept even while Yeager, using the lantern's glow, located and lighted the lamp on the bunkhouse table. Then it was Mitch Starker, feverish and sore from the effects of Yeager's spurring, who stirred and awoke. Startled, he lunged upright, but froze to stillness under the threat of Yeager's gun.

"You can make it as easy or rough as you want," Yeager told him. "But we're moving you fellows out of here."

The other three began stirring and waking, each to know the same surprise, and each, as he recognized the odds of three grim men with drawn and ready guns, made no move or attempt at resistance. But Mitch Starker was surly.

"You're just storin' it up bigger and bigger for yourself, Yeager. You ain't got chips enough to sit into a game like this."

"That, we'll see," Yeager said shortly. "Get the weapons, Jed."

Jed Mims went along, lifting belts and holstered guns off various wall pegs. In a corner by the door a couple of rifles were stacked. These, along with the belt guns, Jed unloaded and laid on an empty bunk.

"Now," he said, "I'll bring in our broncs."

Yeager used the interval until Jed's return, to roll and smoke a cigarette. When Jed reappeared in the bunkhouse door he made brief announcement.

"Daylight's comin' in across the Seminoles. These fellers can see to travel, Gil. And it'll be light enough for us to see that they keep on travelin'."

"Fine!" Yeager said. "Up and on your way, gentlemen."

The combine hands climbed out of their blankets and dressed in silence.

"Take along your warbags," Yeager directed.

"Why?" Mitch Starker said. "We'll be comin' back."

"We'll see about that," retorted Yeager drily. "Move out!"

In the gray, breaking dawn light the combine hands caught and saddled. Climbing stiffly astride, Mitch Starker threw a glance toward the cookshack. Noting the glance, Yeager smiled thinly.

"The cook is resting easy, Starker. And he'll be along, later."

Before reining away, Starker dropped a final surly comment. "Better pray to God your luck holds, Yeager. Because you're sure going to need all of it!"

"Get going!" Yeager shot back. "You talk too damn much."

He watched these men leave, watched their mounted figures sink into the pool of lingering night shadow which lay short of the lift of ground that rose above Rubicon

Creek, until they seemed merely figments of shadow themselves. Afterwards he watched them climb the low slope to emerge on the crest, solid and real and strongly etched against the lightening sky. Then they tipped beyond the crest and were gone, and it was as if something foreign had made welcome exit from his world.

For this was his world. He made a slow, complete turn, pivoting on his bootheels, taking in every familiar item of the headquarters. This was his creation, this he had built. Into this he had put muscle and sweat, weariness and strong purpose. He had lost it and he had regained it, and it was his. His—by God!

"Well," said Alec Trezevant at Yeager's elbow, "so far, so good. That came off a lot quieter than I figured it would. Now I'm wondering how long it will stay quiet? I'm inclined to think Mitch Starker meant it when he said they'd be back."

"They'll be back," Yeager agreed soberly. "I don't know in what way—but they'll be back. They can't afford not to make some sort of try. For one reason, this place has been the source of their strength on the east side of the lake. For another, if they stand for this without putting up a real fight, then they openly admit they've no right to any Summit Prairie range outside their first holding, the old Patrick place. So they'll be back. But we got this on our side. Whenever they do and however they do, they'll be bucking the law. For possession is ours, now—and it is legal possession."

"They come huntin' it," Jed Mims put in succinctly, "they'll find it. They'll get as good as they send, and mebbe a little extra."

They went back to the cookshack and Yeager, as he freed the combine cook, said:

"You can leave any time you want. Starker and the others have pulled out. I'm sorry I had to rough you up some. Nothing personal about it, you understand. It was just that things had to be handled that way."

Sitting on the edge of the bunk, the cook rubbed his wrists

where the thongs had been set. He was a man resigned, with no hostility in him at all, now.

"I don't know the how and why of any of this," he said, his voice husky in his bruised throat. "Like I said before, I'm just a cook. Past that, ranch affairs belong to somebody else. If it is all the same to you, I'd like to stir up a pot of coffee before I pull out."

"Fly to it," Yeager applauded. "That listens good."

It ended up with more than a cup of coffee. It was instead a full, well prepared breakfast, and the four of them ate hungrily. The cook gave his name. It was Pudge Jenkins.

"You sling a mean skillet, my friend," Yeager told him. "I get fully settled and with things quieted down, I could use a man like you in this cookshack. That is, of course, if you're in any way interested."

Jenkins shook his head. "The combine's been payin' my wages. I'll stay with them."

"Good enough," Yeager nodded. "I can respect any good man who stays true to his hire."

A little later Pudge Jenkins rode away on an ancient old pony, his warbag and other gear tied to his saddle.

"There," observed Jed Mims, looking after the departing figure, "goes a little cuss I think I could come to like."

9.

To THE LIMIT such a thing could be in one of his acid, generally humorless nature, Sheriff Kline Hyatt was swayed by vast inner amusement. Accompanying this emotion that was, to him, relatively foreign, was a measure of cynical satisfaction.

He sat in his office chair, leaning comfortably back, his dry cheeks expressionless, his eyes narrowed as he squinted through the drift of blue smoke lifting from the tip of his cigar. Now he rolled the cigar from one corner of his mouth to the other and spoke past it.

"I've told you this before, Bastian. You get a warrant sworn out of Judge Carmody's court and I'll serve it. Without that—well—" He shrugged.

Three others were present. Ollie Ladd stood beside the door, dark and brooding, uncertainty in his heavy glance as it shuttled between Hyatt and Meade Bastian, who was striding back and forth across the meager limits of the room, a repressed anger showing in his every move and word. On the edge of the room's only other chair, Mitch Starker sat gingerly, holding himself rigidly erect, grimacing every time he stirred under the pain of lacerated, stiffened muscles.

Meade Bastian hauled to a stop in front of the desk and laid the pale weight of his glance on Hyatt.

"The last time we talked you crawled behind that same damn flimsy excuse, Hyatt; that you had to have a warrant out of Carmody's court before you could act. To hell with that sort of guff! You don't need a warrant to get along out there and boot Yeager off that ranch."

"And just what," Hyatt murmured, "would I charge him with? What would I offer for reason or cause?"

Bastian waved an impatient arm. "There's plenty to charge him with. I'm telling you that he and Mims and old man Trezevant went in there, threw guns on Starker here, and the rest of our men, and run them off the place under the threat of those guns. What more cause or reason do you need than that?"

A ghost of that inner amusement became a bleak gleam in Kline Hyatt's eyes.

"If," he said, with slow distinctness, "such a thing came easier to me, I'd be laughing myself sick, Bastian. When I think of the high and mighty way all you combine buckos have swaggered up and down this prairie, and now to hear you wail and whine because somebody beats you at your own game of take it and keep it—why, yeah, that sure does make for a long, loud laugh. Only—," and here Hyatt came upright in his chair and gave his words a forward-leaning emphasis, "when you played rough you were outside the law, while what friend Yeager did last night he had a perfect right to do."

"Right to do!" gritted Bastian. "What do you mean—right to do?"

"Just that. All he did was to boot some trespassers off a piece of ranch property which is morally and legally his. Show me any court in the land—any honest court, I mean, not one such as Elias Blackmur might preside over—that would class what Yeager did as a criminal action. If you think Judge Carmody would regard it as such, go make your complaint to him. I think I'd rather enjoy being present when you do."

Savagely angry though he was, Meade Bastian was shrewd enough to know when it was time to try a change in tactics. So he caged his anger as best he could and adopted a more placating tone and manner.

"You're a practical man, Hyatt. You've been on our side in the past and we've made it worth your while. You keep playing along with us and we'll make it more so in the future. We'll even—"

"Hold it!" broke in Hyatt curtly. "I'm way too old to believe in fairy stories. Neither do I enjoy being played as a fool. You say you took care of me in the past, made everything worth my while. How, Bastian—how? I'll tell you how. By holding the club of political pressure over my head. By talk of votes to be swung for me or against me. Well, I used to think that sort of thing counted, that it was important. I find now that it isn't—not a bit!"

He leaned back in his chair again and drew deeply on his cigar before resuming.

"A mistake people like you make, Bastian, is to figure other men haven't any pride; that you can push them around, tromp all over them and that they'll still come up smiling and loving you. Yeah, that they never heard of such a thing as pride. Well, strangely enough, I find I got some, considerably more than I once thought. And I like the fact. Also and besides, I like the feeling of being up off my hands and knees and on my feet again. That fact, Bastian, I like to beat all hell!"

Listening, Meade Bastian lost the fight to hide his true feelings under a cloak of persuasive blandness. The anger in him blazed through again, his pale eyes taking on a flaring blankness, the flat, hard pull of his lips bracketing his mouth with deep-furrowed lines.

"So you've gone completely over to the other side, eh, Hyatt?"

"To another side," nodded Hyatt coolly. "But not the one you mean. The side I'm on now plays it right up the middle. I told you that before, you and Duke Royale."

Bastian laid the full weight of that blank, pale stare on the sheriff, and Hyatt met it unwaveringly. Bastian swung away.

"Come on, Mitch," he growled to Starker. Short of the door he stopped, confronting Ollie Ladd, who had held his position there in ponderous silence, scowling and blinking as he tried to follow the play of words between Hyatt and Bastian, and to wring from them their true meaning.

"Ollie, how about you?" Bastian demanded. "Where do you stand? With us, or with Hyatt? You were our man before you was his, remember. So, what's it to be, now?"

"That," murmured Kline Hyatt, getting to his feet and moving past the desk, "is a good question, Bastian. In fact, one I was intending to ask of Ollie, myself. You couldn't have picked a better time and place. And you're making it plain that there can be no middle ground, no neutral stand. It must be either for or against. Well, that's all right with me. We'll see how it is with Ollie. Speak up, Ollie. The man has asked you a question. He's waiting for your answer. I want to hear it, myself."

Ollie Ladd swung his glance from one to the other of these two men now making flat demand for his stand on loyalty. One of them he understood much better than he did the other. For during the past day or two, Kline Hyatt had been voicing some distinctions on attitude and conduct that were more than a little confusing to Ollie. There was no flexibility to Ollie's mind; what thinking he managed was grooved, and once he got an angle finally worked out to his own satisfaction, that, where he was concerned, was the way it had to be.

Before Hyatt, under pressure from the combine, had made him deputy, Ollie had ridden for the combine as an ordinary cowhand. That the sole reason for this promotion was due to the fact that the combine saw in him a dull and ruthless brutishness that would take orders and follow them to the letter, was something that had never occurred to Ollie. And the satisfaction he had known in wearing a deputy's star was almost childlike. As Ollie saw it, the man who wore a star walked with the mighty.

But now Ollie was confused, upset. The way the combine did things was the way he liked to do them. Push straight ahead, and if anybody got in your way, knock him down and tramp over him. Or, if you figured he needed killing—kill him. . . .

For a long time, whatever the combine wanted, was, it seemed, all right with Kline Hyatt. But now Hyatt had changed. He was arguing with the combine, going stubborn, and for reasons which Ollie couldn't understand and didn't in his eyes, make good sense.

Ollie's swinging glance finally settled and held on Kline Hyatt, and Ollie blurted things as he saw them.

"This Yeager—what's he to us? We'd had a little more luck, we'd have hung that feller. He's no friend of ours. But Bastian, here, and Mitch and the rest of the combine fellers, they're on our side and we're on theirs. We drink with them in Duke Royale's place, and—"

"Just a minute," broke in Hyatt crisply. He had moved within a stride of this dark, hulking fellow, and now considered him with a narrow bleakness. "That is the only way you see it, Ollie? Doesn't the question of right or wrong, of what's inside or outside of the law enter at all? You see it

97

only as who you think are your friends, or your enemies? Is that as far as you've got this thing figured?"

Under the impact of Hyatt's rapid-fire questions, Ollie's befuddlement and confusion grew. But he clung doggedly to the only point that made sense to him.

"How else you goin' to figure it?" he mumbled. "If you ain't for your friends, who are you for?"

"That's it, Ollie!" put in Meade Bastian. "That's laying it right on the line."

Kline Hyatt paid no attention to Bastian or his remark. He stepped close to Ollie, reached with a swift lift of his hand for the star pinned to Ollie's shirt. He caught this and jerked it and with a short rip of cloth brought it away. He stepped back and tossed the star on his desk.

"Ollie," he said, "you stand just too damn far to one side to go on wearing that. Now you can go back to punching cows for your combine friends."

Ollie Ladd stared down at the small tear in his shirt marking the spot where his star had been. Slowly his glance came back up and fixed on Kline Hyatt. Ollie's massive shoulders hunched and a feral growl erupted gutturally in his throat. He rolled up on his toes as if to launch himself forward in a headlong rush.

Kline Hyatt fixed him with a narrow alertness.

"Don't try it, Ollie. You'd never get there!"

The growl died in Ollie's throat and he settled back on his heels again. Hyatt jerked an indicating head.

"Clear out—all of you! And get rid of any idea you may have of threatening or bluffing this office. Because that sort of thing just won't go!"

Meade Bastian took Ollie Ladd by the arm, hauled him around and steered him through the door into the hall. Mitch Starker limped after them. Kline Hyatt listened to the sounds of departure and when all was quiet, went slowly back to his chair. He fingered the star he'd stripped off Ollie Ladd, stared at it for a moment, then tossed it into a desk drawer.

His cigar had gone dead. He scratched a match, nursed

this to full flame, carefully relit his smoke. Then he lay back in his chair and for the next quarter hour considered a number of things. Presently, with some abruptness, he got to his feet, a man come to decision. He left the office and climbed the steps to the upper reaches of the courthouse, hoping to find Judge Carmody in his chambers. In this he was successful. The Judge was busy at a desk piled high with weighty law tomes.

The Judge's greeting was tart. "Something I can do for you, Sheriff?"

Hyatt nodded. "I'd like a little of your time, Judge. I've a few things to get off my mind. Somewhat in the nature of a confessional."

"Well, well!" rumbled the Judge in his deepest tones, a gleam of quickening interest in his eyes. "They do say that such a thing is good for the soul. Sheriff, I give you my entire attention."

It was a full hour later before Kline Hyatt moved to leave. Judge Carmody accompanied him to the door. The Judge's manner had mellowed considerably and in the regard he placed on Hyatt lay a definite leavening of respect.

"I would suggest, Sheriff, that we consider first things first. We know that Gil Yeager did not kill Cress Lucas. But obviously, somebody did. Lucas was shot in the back?"

Hyatt nodded. "In the back."

"Which makes it murder, of course. The trail is bound to be cold. But do the best you can."

Kline Hyatt returned to his own office. He unlocked a lower drawer of his desk, and from beneath a stack of time yellowed official letter-heads, brought out a number of reward 'dodgers'—notices of wanted men. These he went over carefully, finally selecting three which he studied at some length. From these, into a small notebook, he copied certain items of information. After . which he returned dodgers and letter-heads to the drawer and relocked it.

Next door to the office along the hall was a small store-room, cluttered with a miscellany of gear. It held a corner closet and from this Hyatt brought out a scabbarded rifle and a holstered Colt six-shooter, wrapped around with a cartridge belt. He took off his coat, unbuckled the harness of the short-barreled shoulder-holstered gun he'd been carrying, hung this in the closet, then strapped the big Colt gun about his lank middle. He settled belt and holstered gun to his liking, donned his coat again, took the scabbarded rifle under his arm and went out into the street, heading for its lower reaches where stood Johnny Hock's freight, stage and livery corrals.

For one whose ordinary posture had been a somewhat stooped slouch, Sheriff Kline Hyatt now walked fairly erect, head and shoulders squared, the usual acid discontent of his expression replaced by a sober sternness, the look of a man who had found a new serenity of mind.

Barney Flood, ambling over from his saddle shop to Patch Kelly's store for a fresh plug of chewing tobacco, found Patch about to start his daily sweeping chore. The tobacco purchase completed, the pair of them now stood on the store porch in the pleasant slant of morning's sunlight, Patch leaning on his broom, Barney carefully paring off a corner of his tobacco plug. As Kline Hyatt came even with them, both went still for a staring moment. Then Patch said:

"Morning, Kline."

Barney also tried a greeting, but managed only a wet mumble past the chew he'd just cheeked.

Hyatt did not pause, merely half lifted a hand, while inclining his head slightly.

"Gentlemen!"

They gazed after him, Barney finally making intelligible speech.

"Son-of-a-gun! Now where would he be goin'? And who after? Somehow he looks different than usual, not like the same man."

His glance still following the on-striding sheriff, a musing light came into Patch Kelly's eyes.

"I don't know who he's after, Barney, but I know who he's found."

"Who'd that be?"

"Himself."

Fifteen minutes later, astride a line-backed dun gelding, Kline Hyatt rode out of town, taking the east side prairie road and heading north along this.

At the Lazy Y, Gil Yeager and Jed Mims toiled at cleaning up the ranchhouse. One room alone showed evidence of fairly regular occupancy, containing a made up bunk and some extra clothes hanging on wall pegs. The balance of the place, aside from the accumulated dust and cobwebs of a year of disuse, was pretty much as it had been when Yeager left it.

"It's in better shape than I thought it would be," he observed. "Looks like only one man stays here. The rest make it in the bunkhouse."

"Probably Meade Bastian's hangout when he decides to stay the night here," Jed Mims said. "As for the rest, there'd be no point or sense in the combine knocking things to pieces. Not when they had it all figured they were set here for good."

While speaking, Jed was brushing some cobwebs from a window. Glancing through the cleared glass, he went sharply alert.

"Rider comin', Gil!"

They moved to the door and Yeager stepped out. Jed stood in the open portal, close to the rifle stacked handily just inside.

"It's Hyatt," identified Yeager.

"Now what would he be wantin'?" Jed wondered. "Been a long time since I saw him on a horse."

"Maybe he's going to run us off the place."

"And maybe he ain't," growled Jed grimly. "He tries, he won't get far."

"That's right," Yeager murmured, as much to himself as

for Jed's ears. "For I'm all done being pushed around by any one-sided law."

They waited and watched while Kline Hyatt brought his line-backed dun in at a jog. When he hauled up before the ranchhouse and took swift account of what he saw, a flicker of amusement showed briefly in his glance and he spoke drily.

"No need staying so damned close to a rifle, Mims. Today I'm harmless."

"Well mebbe you are," said Jed. "But you didn't ride out here just for the hell of it."

"No," Hyatt admitted, "I didn't. I'm looking for information and thought I might pick some up." He looked at Yeager. "How's it seem to be back on your own land again?"

"Good," Yeager told him briefly. Puzzled, Yeager studied Hyatt intently, trying to figure him, trying to account for the definitely startling change in the man. A hostility always present before, was not there now. Where there had been a certain suggestion of shiftiness, there was now a steadiness, a reassuring impression of solidity. "This information you're after," Yeager added slowly, "it's about last night?"

Hyatt shook his head. "I know all about last night. I understand you ran some trespassers off your place."

"That's putting it fair enough," Yeager agreed with some caution. "Mitch Starker seemed to feel they'd be back. If they try, things could shape up rough."

"That's right," Hyatt nodded, "they could. Because any man has the right to defend his own property."

Yeager drew a deep, slow breath, his eyes narrowing. His words ran blunt.

"Hyatt, I don't get this. You trying to tell me something?"

Hyatt shrugged. "Not particularly. Just making general observation. If it's all right with you I'm getting out of this saddle for a few minutes. I've done damn little riding in the past six months and I find I'm saddle soft."

Hyatt swung down, stamped his heels against the ground several times, shook his shoulders and sighed his relief.

Marking the gun at the sheriff's hip, Jed Mims stirred restlessly in the ranchhouse doorway. Kline Hyatt looked at him, without amusement now, and his words struck crisply.

"I told you to forget that rifle, Mims! If I was out here after somebody, it wouldn't make a damn bit of difference if you had a dozen weapons stacked around. I'd still collar my man. You ought to know that." He turned to Yeager. "What I want to see you about is the Cress Lucas affair. Now hold on—don't get spooky! It's agreed and accepted and official that you had nothing to do with that killing. What I want from you is an opinion, should you have one, of who might have done it. You've no doubt done a lot of thinking on the matter. Have you come up with any kind of an idea that makes sense?"

Instead of an answer, Yeager had a question of his own. "Who's trying to dig that thing up again?"

"Not who—what," Hyatt told him. "It's the law that wants to know. Cress Lucas was shot in the back. Why, or by whom, I don't know. But of one thing I'm sure. It was murder. And it is Judge Carmody's desire, and my own, that the killer be brought to justice."

"Kinda late, ain't it, to be worryin' about that?" asked Jed Mims from the doorway. "There's a trail a year old and a year cold. Time you should have dug into it, Hyatt, was right when it happened, instead of tryin' to saddle it on to Gil Yeager, an innocent man."

Kline Hyatt's answer was so grave and quiet it left Jed wordless, his mouth open in disbelief.

"You're right, Mims. That was as it should have been. However, in the clearing of Yeager's name, part of that miscarriage of justice has been rectified. But the real killer is still running loose, and, cold as the trail may be, I'm out to find the beginning of it." Again his glance swung to Yeager. "I'd still like your opinion if you have one."

Yeager shook his head. "I can't offer a thing, Hyatt. I wasn't anywhere near Burnt Corral either before or after the killing. The first I knew of it was when I was arrested and charged with it."

"Maybe," suggested Hyatt, "when you came up with Shad Emmett in Two Rivers and got the confession of perjury out of him, he might have said something that would offer a lead?"

Again Yeager shook his head. "Not a thing that I recall. If he had, I'd sure as hell have remembered."

Jed Mims came away from the door and began spinning up a cigarette.

"Mebbe you should ask some of that combine crowd about the Lucas killing, Hyatt."

"And maybe I will," Hyatt said. "Well, I'll be getting along. If either of you should come up with a theory that makes sense, let me know."

He turned to his horse and climbed into the saddle a little stiffly. Yeager, still pondering the startling difference in this man Kline Hyatt, and completely at sea to account for it, moved over and looked up at him gravely.

"I'm still fighting my head, Hyatt—trying to figure you. Because you're—well, God damn it, man, acting the part of a real sheriff now, instead of playing stooge to the combine."

Faintly smiling again, Hyatt held Yeager's glance for a moment. Then he lifted his gaze to the far, smoky upsurge of the Seminoles.

"Glad it's so apparent, Yeager. The change, I mean. It was meant to be, so there'd be no mistaking it by anyone."

Saying which, Sheriff Kline Hyatt nodded brief farewell, swung his horse and jogged away.

10.

IT WAS NEARING sundown when Alec and Anita Trezevant rode in, leading a pair of burdened packhorses. While Jed Mims helped old Alec care for the horses, Gil Yeager showed Anita into the ranchhouse. He smiled down at her and waved an encircling hand.

"Your territory. Jed and I did some cleaning up. You won't find it too bad."

She looked about her, pleasure shining in her dark eyes, her lips softening to a gentle smiling.

"It will be good to be in a house again, even if it isn't my own," she said simply. "Just to be under a roof once more and to have a real kitchen to cook in. This is very generous of you, Gil."

"Stuff!" he scoffed. "We're all partners in a common cause." Somewhat soberly, he added, "I'll worry some."

"About what?"

"You. If the combine has a try at regaining this place—and they're almost sure to—then things could turn rough and some shooting start."

"Now I say—stuff!" she retorted. "Father will be here. So will you and Jed. I'm not afraid."

Along with a warm, serene beauty, this girl had moral fiber and courage and the strength of a vitally independent spirit. She wouldn't, Yeager thought, ever be afraid of anything. . . .

Throughout the day, Yeager and Jed Mims had not relaxed their watchfulness for a moment. At no time were their weapons other than handy to their reach. For it was as Gil had explained to Anita Trezevant; the combine was certain to strike back in some way.

They virtually had to. The word was sure to be out now, and would travel fast. It would reach the deepest corner of the Chinkapin country, where discouraged men would hear how Gil Yeager, in one bold surprise move had regained his ranch. In this fact these same men might very well find new will to strike in their own behalf.

The one certain way the combine could head off such re-action was to demonstrate they still had too much power and weight to combat successfully. To demonstrate this fact, they had to regain possession of the Lazy Y.

These facts Yeager discussed at length with Jed Mims and Alec Trezevant.

"They'll outnumber us," he emphasized. "And if I read that fellow Meade Bastian right, they won't give a thin damn how rough they get. And if they gain a foothold, we're done. So we guard, day and night. With just three of us, that won't be easy. But if we can hang on and make things stick for a while, we should begin getting a little help here and there."

"Maybe," growled Alec Trezevant pessimistically. "I wouldn't count on it, though. Best way to figure is the three of us against the world. Then we'll know exactly where we stand. I'll take the late night watch. I don't sleep too good after midnight, anyhow."

"Here's another point," Yeager said, lips pursed in soberness. "Understand, Anita is more than welcome here. But I hate to think of her facing any slightest risk of any kind. Do you think we could persuade her to go stay in town until this thing is settled?"

Old Alec snorted. "Not a chance! Why, right after we lost our ranch I tried to get her to go stay with Maggie Spelle at the hotel in town. Did she light into me for even suggesting such a thing!" Pride touched his lips with a grim smile. "Since then she's siwashed it with me all through the Seminoles, taking the bitter with the sweet—and there's been a hell of a lot of the first and damn little of the second. Besides, Bastian won't dare get rough with her. He does, then I forget everything else and hunt him down like I would a mad wolf. And to hell with the consequences!"

With a full hour of leeway before having to start supper, Anita had heated a wash tub of water and enjoyed the luxury of a hot bath. Afterwards, from her personal gear, she brought forth a gingham house dress which she now wore with simple effectiveness. The satisfaction of returning fully to feminine attire, plus the warmth of the kitchen stove, had deepened the color in her face and there was the shine of pure contentment in her eyes when she called the men in for the evening meal. Looking at her across the table, Jed Mims spoke with gentle humor.

"Girl, you're prettier than a spotted pup. Wish I was forty years younger."

The glow in her dusky cheeks deepened and she showed old Jed the bright goodness of her smile.

The shadow of something far, far away, flickered momentarily in Alec Trezevant's deep-set, black eyes.

" 'Minds me of her ma," he said softly.

Agreeing fully with Jed Mims' opinion of beauty, Gil Yeager now wondered about something which had existed back in the good days before the blight of combine greed and conquest had hit this high prairie world. He remembered Burke Benedict and Anita Trezevant as he had seen them together on various occasions; a chance meeting in town, or riding along a trail somewhere, or at one of the dances in the loft of Patch Kelly's warehouse. And at such times there was that in the manner with which these two people would look at each other that put them completely alone in a world standing still and breathless before the wonder of something they alone seemed to see and understand.

But what of that vision, today?

Back at the Coulee Glades camp, Alec Trezevant had said something about Anita and Burke Benedict seeing no more of each other, because of opposed opinions over combine trouble. Burke, apparently, had sought and found friendship of some sort with the combine, while Alec Trezevant had fought it fiercely. And Anita, just as fiercely loyal and strong in spirit, had followed her father.

Made restless by these thoughts, Yeager got out his smoking and grimly frowned as he spun up a cigarette. For memory was taking him back across arid, desperate months to the old, good days when at times he stood before beauty and knew the warmth of its smile.

Laurie Benedict—what of Laurie Benedict . . . ?

He got to his feet, shook his head at Anita's offer of another cup of coffee. To Trezevant he said:

"I'll call you at midnight, Alec."

Jed Mims spoke up swiftly. "A three man chore, this guarding business. Where do I fit in?"

"Tonight you don't," Yeager said. "Get your sleep. There'll be plenty for you to do, tomorrow."

As he donned his coat and stepped out into the night, Jed's grumbling complaint followed him.

"Anybody would think I wasn't a man grown."

He caught and saddled and rode out to the crest of land about Rubicon Creek. Clear of the murk of last night, the early-out stars now burned coldly brilliant. Far up the run of Rubicon Creek a single spark of light marked the Benedict ranch. For a long minute Yeager sat his saddle motionless, observing that distant pinpoint of yellow, while recollection swept through him with a deepening poignancy.

He swung his shoulders, restlessness nagging him. He put his thoughts and gaze to the south, for, that being the short way around the lake from main combine headquarters, attack, when it came, would likely materialize from such direction.

He dropped down to Rubicon Creek, crossed, and sent his horse along at a swinging walk, pausing now and then to test the world about him. The breath of the lake came in over his right shoulder, bringing its wet odors and, faintly, the raucous and plaintive and lonely cries of its feathered folk.

He prowled the prairie to the southern tip of the lake and for a couple of miles beyond, seeing nothing, hearing nothing. Dead ahead, but distant, the lights of town made a low, glittering cluster in the night.

Turning back, he held to the main road and when even with the Benedict ranch cut-off, picked up the mutter of hoofs coming in along it. He swung from the road for a yard or two, waiting until the approaching horse and rider became a shadowy bulk as well as a sound. Then he sent out his call.

"Hello—the night!"

The rider reined up and hit back with sharp, impatient words.

"This is Doctor Parris. Who are you and what the devil do you want?"

"Sorry, Doc. Gil Yeager, here. Just sort of checking the trails." Yeager reined back into the road, recalling Doc Parris as a spare, brisk, snapping-eyed man who, over his years of practice had observed so much human frailty and stupidity, he could afford to be acid-tongued concerning it. "Someone hurt or sick at the Benedict ranch, maybe?"

"Old Dave," Doc Parris answered, his tone mollifying. "He's been slipping away for some time. This afternoon he went into a coma. Cam Reeves like to foundered a horse coming after me. There wasn't a thing I could do. The old fellow was gone by the time I got there. You say you're checking the trails. What for?"

"To see who's riding them."

"Would that mean you're hunting more trouble?"

"Not necessarily. Nothing I want less than trouble."

Doc grunted, then made a crisp retort. "The actions hardly fit the words. I flatter myself I did a pretty fair job on Brick Rand's jaw; but it will never be the same. What did you hit him with, a club? And his belly! That looked like he'd

109

fell out of a tree on to a stack of fence posts. You didn't kick him when you had him down, did you?"

"No, I didn't kick him. I only used my fists. I guess I had a lot of mad stored up and I took some of it out on Rand."

"On Mitch Starker, too, so I hear," Doc said. "He didn't come to me for care, but I understand you used a spur on him. Yes, sir—" drily, "for a man who wants no trouble, you got a damn queer way of showing it."

Doc paused to light his pipe. Then he straightened in his saddle and shook the reins.

"Got to get along and make arrangements to take care of old Dave. They're bringing him in tonight. Funeral tomorrow. Good man, Dave. Benedict was—damn good man. But the shape he was in, it's a blessing he's gone."

"How are Burke and Laurie taking it, Doc?" Yeager asked. "Especially Laurie?"

Doc let out a big drag of smoke. "Sensible. Lot of character behind those two people. Yes, sir—a lot of character. You going to show at the funeral? They'd appreciate it, I think."

"I'll show," Yeager promised.

Doc stirred up his horse. "See you there," he called across his shoulder.

Yeager rode back to the rise above Rubicon Creek, dismounted and settled down on his heels. Overhead the stars wheeled their certain way across night's sky. The spark of light at the Benedict ranch held on and Yeager understood why that would be so. Just before midnight when he was about to seek his saddle again, the light winked out.

Back at headquarters he found Alec Trezevant already stirring about in the bunkhouse. "No sign?" Trezevant asked.

"No sign."

With breakfast's savory odors ripening the air, Alec Trezevant came in from his late guard stint, made taciturn by an old man's early morning grumpiness, his shoulders hunched against the biting chill of the high prairie air. Mellowing over a cup of coffee, he reported nothing untoward during his watch.

"Which," he growled, "don't mean a damn thing. Lots of nights ahead. On one of them we'll have our fun."

Jed Mims nodded. "In their place I wouldn't try to hit back too quick, either. I'd wait until the other fellow turned a mite careless."

"We're not going to turn careless," Gil Yeager said. "Jed, you were stewing about your share of guard watch. Well, it's all yours, now. You got the whole day ahead of you."

"Which means you're up to—what?" grumbled Jed.

"A little moseying, a little looking around."

"During which you could meet up with something. You better let me trail along. Bastian won't be showing here during broad day."

"Maybe not," Yeager admitted. "But we got to believe he might. So you hang around; Alec's got some sleeping to do." He turned to Anita Trezevant. "I may get as far as town, Anita. Anything you want?"

She shook a dark head, gravely smiling. "Nothing, Gil."

Jed followed out to the corrals, watching while Yeager caught and saddled.

"I'd stay clear of town," he warned. "That's enemy territory."

"No," Yeager differed. "Not so, Jed. If we admit that, then we admit the whole prairie is theirs. For myself, I see only one piece of range being combine land—the old Patrick place. Past that, they're the ones off the reservation, not us."

"True enough," agreed Jed. "But they'll be set to argue the point."

Yeager shrugged. "Then they'll have their argument."

From headquarters he rode north along the lake shore, aware of a sense of possession almost physical in its satisfaction. For it seemed that land which a man had once moved across and known to be fully his, carried an invisible impact that could reach up and touch him when once again

111

he traveled it. This was so, even though long months lay between past and present contact, months, mused Yeager, during which he had several times doubted he'd ever see this land again, much less ride across it and feel its vigor come up to him. Yet, here it was beneath him, and it was his!

He began moving cattle, and though he looked them over carefully, on none did he see a Lazy Y brand, vented or otherwise. Most wore the combine's Sixty-six iron, with here and there a critter carrying Burke Benedict's Long B. Regardless of possible significance in this fact—or lack of it— sight of combine and Benedict cattle grazing together across his land, pulled Yeager's lips to a line of harshness. For in spite of all generous reasoning, and of allowances being made, this thing suggested persistent and disturbing possibilities.

Had the cattle been Long B alone, he wouldn't have cared. But combine cattle along with Long B, that was something else again. It was, he decided, something he had every right to ask a few pointed questions about.

Last night Doc Parris had said Dave Benedict would be buried today, and it was reasonable to guess the funeral would not take place before noon, or after. So, while Burke and Laurie Benedict were probably in town, someone, maybe Cam Reeves, should still be at the ranch, what with morning not too far along. Cam Reeves, as Yeager remembered him, was a sound, reliable man. And from him, he'd glean a few enlightening answers.

Yeager swung away from the lake shore, cutting east toward the Seminoles, the far crests of which ran sharp-edged against the sunrise sky. But the lower flank of the hills and the rocky depths of gulch and canyon still lay blue and cold in a veil of morning mist.

He crossed the dusty ribbon of the road and slanted south, presently striking a considerable run of north pasture fence. This he skirted to a gate, which he opened and closed from the saddle, afterwards splashing across Rubicon Creek to pull up at the Long B ranchhouse.

His first thought was that he'd guessed wrong about possible occupancy of the ranch, everything was so quiet and seemingly empty. But now the ranchhouse door opened and it was Laurie Benedict who stood before him.

She was dressed in black and there were signs of recent tears about her eyes, but she was slim and still and composed. She had, Yeager thought, met and mastered the first impact of her natural grief. He reached up and hauled off his hat.

"I didn't figure to disturb you, Laurie. I thought you'd be in town, but that perhaps Cam Reeves would be around. I met Doc Parris along the road last night and he told me about your uncle. I'm sorry to hear of it."

She acknowledged this word of sympathy with a slight tip of her head.

"He was an old, old man," she said simply. "He had lived a long time. He went quietly to sleep, dying peacefully in his own bed, under his own roof, on his own land. It—it was the way he wished the end to come, so Burke and I wished it that way, too." She paused, as if to contemplate something before adding, almost defiantly, "We've no regrets, Burke and I. What we have done, and how we did it, we saw merely as our duty to Uncle Dave." She paused again, then said, "You mentioned Cam Reeves. He's not here just now. There was something you wanted?"

"I had some questions in mind when I came here," Yeager admitted a little lamely, "but they seem to have lost their importance. It is good to see you again, Laurie—to talk with you."

Faint color warmed her wan cheeks. She studied him, marking the vast change in this man she had once known so well. A year ago there had been a rather round and careless casualness about him, a manner to attract because of its cheerfulness and easy going acceptance of life's inevitable vagaries. But there had been some who argued this manner could cast doubt on a man's basic worth, and proclaim him soft.

Well, there was no softness in him now. He was rawhide

lean and rawhide tough. His jaw was hard-angled almost to boniness, and his lips carried a pressure at their corners that edged them with a shadowy harshness. His eyes, deep set, were frosted with a wary reserve. Here, she realized, was a man who had had all semblance of his former easy acceptance of life driven completely out of him. The change had made him older and, in some strange way, increased his stature.

She recalled those wicked moments in front of Patch Kelly's store when this same Gil Yeager had battered Brick Rand to a retching, helpless, shattered hulk, and while the spectacle had to a certain degree sickened her, it had also held her fascinated by its raw brutality and utter ruthlessness. At the time—and since—she had thought that any man so reverted to pure savagery, would never fully emerge from such state again. Yet, here he was, right before her, straight and balanced and watching her with a grave and gentle respect.

"You're considering a number of things, all with reservation," he observed shrewdly. "Well, I don't blame you. Since I've returned, you haven't seen me in a very decent light. I'd ask a little patience of you, Laurie. For I've quite a few things to forget, and much to remember. The remembering comes easiest. For it takes in all the good times we had together in the old days."

The color in her cheeks deepened as she searched for a reply. Before she could find one there came the splash of hoofs and the grate of steel shod wheels over rocks, and Yeager twisted in his saddle to see Cam Reeves bring the ranch buckboard across the ditch at the mouth of the south lane. The team, despite the run out from town, was still full of morning's vigor, and they brought the light rig briskly across the interval to a swinging stop before the ranchhouse porch. Riding the brake, Cam Reeves said:

"Any time you're ready, Laurie."

"Right away, Cam," she answered, turning back into the house.

Cam looped the reins about the brake handle, got out a

blackened pipe and stoked it carefully. He scratched a match and past the first mouthful of smoke, studied Yeager keenly.

"Kline Hyatt was by here yesterday mornin'. Told us about you being back on your old stamping grounds. You figure to make it stick?"

"Figure to try."

Cam mused over this a moment, then nodded. "Wish you luck. But don't take a damn thing for granted. There ain't nothin' I'd put past Meade Bastian and Duke Royale."

"Duke Royale?"

"Feller who runs the Golden Horn," said Cam. "There's some who think all he's interested in is that deadfall. Not me. More to him than that. Him and Bastian are as thick as any pair of thieves can get. And sometimes I think mebbe they're closer than that, even. Should you get a chance to see them together, take a good look. See what answer you come up with. A pair of bad ones, those two, and they could be out of the same litter."

"This spread seems to get along with them pretty well," Yeager observed drily. "For I see Long B stock grazing side by side with Sixty-six stuff on my land. What am I to think?"

Cam's leathery cheeks crimsoned and quick anger flared in his eyes.

"Think anything you damn please!" Then quickly, shaking his head, he added, "No, I didn't mean that. You got a good question there, and you're entitled to a good answer. Like others, you're thinking and guessing at a lot of things, and you're all wrong as hell. There's a big change coming up. I suggest you wait and take a good look at it before passing any judgment."

Laurie Benedict came out of the house again. She had donned a long linen duster over her black dress and wore a small black hat and black veil.

As she crossed toward the rig, Yeager was swiftly out of his saddle, giving her an aiding hand up to the buckboard seat. From the eminence of this she looked down at him, but whatever her face held was hidden by her veil. She murmured something he did not catch. Then Cam Reeves, picking up his reins, kicked off the brake, clucked to his team, and the buckboard spun away.

Yeager stared after the departing rig, marking the slim, erect grace of Laurie's trim shoulders. To him again in full tide came all the feeling he'd once known for this girl and it was a stronger, more compelling thing than it had ever been.

He went back into the saddle, lifted his horse to a jog, heading for town.

11.

"You, I UNDERSTAND, have been more or less raising hell and putting a rock under it," said Johnny Hock. "While you were scrambling here and yon on the trail of Shad Emmett, you must have been feeding on raw meat."

"To the contrary, John," Gil Yeager answered drily. "I wasn't eating often enough. That's what soured my disposition."

"Well, you must have been doing a lot better at the table than when I saw you last," observed Johnny. "Not quite so much of that gaunt, slab-sided look to you—like your clothes were too big for you. Damn! I'd sure liked to have been on hand when you cut Brick Rand down to size. But of course I would have to be in Gardnerville closing that freighting deal with Walt Haley. On top of that you work Mitch Starker over with a spur and then kick the combine off your ranch. I'm wondering whether you're lucky or mean—or both, Gil?"

Yeager grinned. "Call it lucky."

They were sitting in Johnny Hock's office, killing time until eleven o'clock, when, so the word was, Dave Benedict would be buried.

Lying back in his chair, Johnny Hock considered the office ceiling soberly.

"You realize of course, my friend, that this could be just the start of things—a lot of things. The combine isn't going to take this lying down. They can't afford to. Maybe you got something more up your sleeve?"

Yeager shook his head. "I'm just reaching from day to day; playing my hand, you might say, one card at a time. I've made my move. Next one is theirs."

"One thing," Johnny Hock said, "you won't have Kline Hyatt working with the combine against you. I visited with Judge Carmody last night and he tells me Hyatt's had a change of heart; that from here on out he's going to run his sheriff's office as it should be, strictly impartial, playing no favorites."

"I'll wait and hope on that," Yeager said skeptically. "I'm wondering if it's really a change of heart, or just another shrewd swing before what Hyatt figures is the present political wind. I admit the man has a new look in his eye, but you got to wonder about such things."

"Terence Carmody seems to feel Hyatt is sincere," Johnny Hock insisted. He looked at his watch and got to his feet. "If we're going to pay our last respects to Dave Benedict, we better be moving."

The cemetery was a short quarter mile from town, out along the Gardnerville road, and the funeral cortege was already pacing slowly toward it when Gil Yeager and Johnny Hock emerged on the street. Johnny Hock had a buckboard hitched and ready for the occasion and now he and Yeager climbed into the rig, Johnny taking the reins. Rolling up street to where the Gardnerville road cut away from town just beyond the courthouse, they had a chance to look over several riders grouped before the Golden Horn.

"Combine men," Johnny Hock murmured. "Watch yourself, Gil. Don't be suckered into any play where they can call the turns. Were I you, I'd get out of town as soon as this funeral is done with."

"Not me," Yeager said briefly. "I quit running some time ago."

"That's not playing it smart," argued Johnny Hock.

"Then I'll play it stupid," retorted Yeager. "I tell you, John—I'm done with running."

It was a quite respectable gathering, there in the frugal little cemetery. Oldtimers from about town were on hand, men like Patch Kelly and Barney Flood and Jake Dolwig, who had known Dave Benedict in the early, good years. Then there was Judge Carmody and his wife, who had ridden out in a spring wagon with Bill and Maggie Spelle from the Summit House Hotel. Now, as the Judge stood at the head of the grave and spoke a few quiet, deep rolling words of eulogy, Mrs. Carmody and Maggie Spelle took Laurie Benedict between them, ready to comfort her if need be.

But this slender girl in black had shed her tears, made her own farewells in her own way, and now she stood, still and strong and contained.

Burke Benedict stood beside Judge Carmody, a big, gaunt figure of a man, frowning and intent of face.

It was soon done with. This was a land of simplicity in such things. Man was born to live the span allotted him by the fates, then go his spiritual way. And if he had lived well and decently, then his grave would be an honorable one. So it was with Dave Benedict.

The various rigs rolled back to town. Johnny Hock let Gil Yeager off in front of Patch Kelly's store and again voiced his warning.

"Now that's over with, Gil, I still think you'd be wise if you'd drift out of town."

Yeager shook his head. "No, John. It's like I told Jed Mims this morning at the ranch. If I concede town as being combine ground, then I got to concede the whole damn prairie as likewise. And damned if I do either! When you put your rig away, come on over to the Lodgepole and I'll buy you a drink."

Johnny Hock started to shake his team into movement again, then held up for a final remark.

"Something I forgot to mention. Did you know that Kline Hyatt had fired Ollie Ladd as deputy, and that Ollie is trailing around with Meade Bastian like a surly dog with a master? Well, that's the word."

Johnny Hock drove on toward his stables and corrals and Yeager stood on Patch Kelly's porch, spinning up a smoke. Johnny Hock's parting words had jolted him, and now, as he watched the play of movement through town, he pondered them and their possible significance. If Ollie Ladd was truly no longer a part of Kline Hyatt's office, then he must be accepted as even more dangerous and unpredictable than before, for now he would be lacking even the moderately restraining influence of a deputy's badge.

Up street, Yeager saw Laurie Benedict go into the hotel with Maggie Spelle, and then Patch Kelly and Jake Dolwig and Barney Flood came along together and moved to reopen their places of business again. Jangling a handful of keys, Patch Kelly paused for a moment beside Yeager.

"Now," said Patch softly, "I looked carefully out there where we were. And I saw nothing of Meade Bastian. It has been my thought that the man was more than passing friendly with Burke and Laurie Benedict. So, unless my thought has been wrong, Bastian has shown small consideration in staying away."

"From what I've heard and seen of Meade Bastian," Yeager said tersely, "the only funeral he's interested in is his own, and it's the only one he'll ever go to."

Patch Kelly shot Yeager a quick glance. "And was there a special meaning behind those words?"

"It's the Irish in you, Patch, imagining things," said Yeager.

"To be sure, to be sure," Patch murmured, turning away to unlock his door and go inside.

Now the Long B buckboard, with Cam Reeves driving and Burke Benedict beside him, came along the street and turned in at the store hitch rail. When he stepped from the rig, Burke Benedict looked at Yeager.

"Obliged for your showing up, Gil. It's appreciated, especially if you came because you wanted to."

"That's it, Burke," Yeager nodded. "I came because I wanted to."

Burke stepped up on the porch. Observing him closely, Yeager saw a subtle, but distinct difference in this big man from the last time they stood face to face. Then, Burke had shown a trapped, harried look, an uncertainty, an atmosphere of frustration, as might a strong man whose strength was crying to be free of the confines of some sort of invisible bonds.

Today that atmosphere of feverish confinement was gone. While Burke was gravely sober and the strength within him quiescent, he moved and spoke with certainty, his tone crisp, his eyes clear and challenging.

"Cam tells me you were at the ranch this morning, wondering about things. Such as Long B cows running with Sixty-six stuff on your range. Well, you got a perfect right to wonder. A lot of people have wondered. There's an answer, of course. Now, while I'm not the sort to go around shouting I'm a martyr, or pretending I'm annointed with the oil of nobility, the fact is that Laurie and me, we had a debt to pay. To a kind and worthy man, the man we just buried."

Burke paused a moment as though to marshal his thoughts, then went on.

"Over a year ago, when Uncle Dave first began to really fail, Laurie and me were thinking of taking him out to the hospital at Gardnerville for treatment. Then Doc Parris told us if we did so, we'd only hurry the end; that off his own land Uncle Dave wouldn't last a month. Doc said some men drew a mysterious strength from land that had long been theirs and which they had been close to, and that Uncle Dave was such a man. Now, that may not make sense to you, Gil—but it is what Doc Parris made Laurie and me believe."

"I believe it, too," Yeager said quietly. "I know exactly what Doc meant."

"Then the rest will make sense to you, too," Burke said. "I've given you the situation Laurie and me were faced with when the combine struck. Except for Hans Ogaard's place way up toward the north end of the prairie, yours and ours were the only outfits on the east side of the lake. Almost before we realized it, Ogaard was squeezed out, you were behind bars and the combine had moved in on your spread. They had us jammed in against the Seminoles, virtually powerless against their numbers.

"Even so, Laurie and me, we might have tried the best fight we knew how, if it hadn't been for Uncle Dave. But we kept thinking of what Doc Parris had told us, and as there wasn't a thing to be gained, realistically considered, in trying to fight then, we made a calculated and limited peace with them. First with Brick Rand, later with Meade Bastian when he came in to take over. Our real purpose may have fooled Rand, but I'm not too sure it did Bastian, for lately he's been showing his teeth at me. Yet our plan worked well enough to gain the end we hoped for, which was that Uncle Dave could live out his final days on his own land, under his own roof."

Again Burke paused, drawing a deep breath, and then his voice ran deep and solid.

"That is all over and done with now, of course, and we Benedicts are ready to show Bastian and his crowd our true feelings and opinions."

From the buckboard, Cam Reeves called sharply.

"Heads up, Burke!"

As did Burke, Gil Yeager looked at Cam, caught his indicating nod. Meade Bastian had joined the group lounging in front of the Golden Horn. He stood a little apart from the others, his feet spread, his shoulders thrown arrogantly back while he stared, pale eyed, at Yeager and Burke. Now he said something to one of his men, who obediently headed for the store, moving up to the end of the porch to deliver his message.

"Meade Bastian wants to see you, Benedict!"

"He's looking right at me, now," Burke retorted. "What more does he want?"

The rider shrugged. "You know damn well what he wants. He wants to see you—where he is! And you better get there, for he's edgy today."

The rider turned away, dragging his spurs.

Cam Reeves said, "Don't go, Burke. Make him come to you."

Burke was still for a brooding moment. Then his head came up. "After today, yes. But I've been wanting to tell that fellow a few things, and in front of his own crowd. There's no time like now!"

Grim with purpose, Burke headed for the Golden Horn. The moment he did so, Meade Bastian wheeled and went into the place, followed by all but two of his men. This pair held their places by the saloon door.

Cam Reeves called again, anxiously.

"No, Burke—no! Don't go in there. Make him come to you!"

But Burke neither paused nor answered, just marched steadily on.

Swearing softly, Cam Reeves jumped from the buckboard and scrambled hurriedly up on to the store porch, fuming.

"With the mood he's in, and set to tell Meade Bastian off, Burke could walk into something. And I would have to leave my gun home today. Loan me yours, Yeager!"

"I'll keep the gun, Cam," Yeager said briefly. "But I've been wanting to see the inside of that deadfall. Come on— we'll back Burke's hand together!"

"I need a gun," blurted Cam. "Give me one minute—!" He darted into the store and from the gun rack grabbed a sawed-off, big bore shotgun, once the pride of a Wells Fargo messenger, but long since traded in to Patch Kelly. There was part of a box of buckshot shells on the shelf beside the stubby, but highly lethal weapon, and Cam, scooping up a handful of these, had the gun broken open and was loading it even as he ran for the door again.

At the far end of the store, Patch straightened and called. "Hey! What the hell goes on?"

"Nothin', I hope!" tossed back Cam over a speeding shoulder. "But should you hear this old equalizer cut loose, you'll know it's plenty!"

By the time Cam was back in the street, Gil Yeager had moved up on the door of the Golden Horn. Of the two men left there by Meade Bastian, one had his shoulders tipped indolently against the front of the place, the other balancing on high heels at the edge of the board sidewalk. They watched Yeager sharply, narrow-lidded challenge in their eyes. Both were armed.

A short stride away, Yeager paused, tipping his head.

"Inside!" he ordered bluntly. "Both of you."

The one leaning against the wall now swung away.

"Hell you say! Mister, who do you think you are?"

"Why," said Yeager bleakly, "I'm the man who prefers your kind in front of me, rather than at my back. You heard me—get inside!"

"Well, well," drawled the rider, sarcastic and still stubborn. "A regular fire-eater come to town, eh?"

"Make that two of them, friend," said Cam Reeves, moving up beside Yeager.

Speaking, Cam dropped the shotgun across the crook of his left arm, his right hand playing with the big, winged hammers of the weapon. Twin muzzles gaped venomously in the general direction of the rider's chest, which individual batted his eyes nervously, then turned in at the doorway.

"Come on, Trip," he said to his companion. "Some things it just don't pay to argue with."

In the Golden Horn the light of midday was subdued; to Gil Yeager it seemed as if an ominous gloom filled the place. Men stood or sat about, some along the bar, a few at the half dozen card tables. Toward its inner end, Meade Bastian was at the bar, along with Duke Royale and Ollie Ladd. Burke Benedict, having walked half way down the room, was paused now, and his voice rang, growling.

"All right, Bastian—here I am. You got anything to say, let's have it. Then it'll be my turn."

Meade Bastian did not answer immediately. He was looking past Burke, his pale, flaring glance on Gil Yeager and Cam Reeves. When he did speak, it was to Duke Royale, his words low and for Royale's ears alone.

Gil Yeager, recalling what Cam Reeves had said to him out at the Long B that morning, made the most of this chance for a careful appraisal of Meade Bastian and Duke Royale as they stood side by side. And he glimpsed something of what Cam had hinted, an approximate height and build, with some similarity of feature, though the opposed coloration of the eyes was a marked physical difference most people would fail to see beyond.

Yeager nodded and murmured, "I get what you meant, Cam."

Stepping past Meade Bastian and Ollie Ladd, Duke Royale came along the room, his glance on Cam Reeves. He indicated the shotgun.

"What's that for—a holdup?"

"If it was, by now you'd be reachin' high," Cam told him pungently. "Either that or spread out cold, plumb full of buckshot."

"If that was supposed to be funny, it wasn't," Duke Royale said acidly. "Take yourself and the cannon outside."

"Later, mebbe," retorted Cam. "Not now. I just came in. As for this"—he patted the shotgun—"I kinda like the old relic. Gives me a comfortable feeling to have hold of it when I'm in a place like this."

Something not far from an ophidian glint lay in Duke Royale's black eyes, but he did not try and press the point, as Meade Bastian finally directed some words at Burke Benedict.

"Would you be traveling with a body guard, Benedict?"

Yeager answered for Burke. "If you mean Reeves and me—this is entirely an idea of our own. I wanted to see what the inside of this place looked like, and Cam—he came along to tell me about it."

"And that's not funny either," said Bastian coldly.

"Who cares?" shrugged Yeager. "The main point is—we're here. And just in case you thought of putting Burke out on some kind of limb, you can figure Cam and me as being right out there with him."

Burke had turned, was looking back at Cam and Yeager. The shadow of a grim smile touched his lips.

"That makes good listening, Gil. Obliged!" Burke turned to Bastian again. "If you got something to say to me, get it off your chest."

"If I were you," Bastian said thinly, "I'd remind myself of a warning you got the other day about turning too friendly with certain people. Things can change damn quick out at the Long B, you know."

"Things have changed, and more than you imagine," Burke said steadily. "So your warnings don't mean a thing any more. And if that's your say, now here's mine. Stay away from me and mine. Don't cross Long B ground again—ever! That goes for you and your whole damn thieving crew!"

On the heels of Burke's flatly defiant ultimatum a distinct moment of dead silence held. Then a long sigh drifted through the room. Duke Royale turned his bitter-black glance on Burke, and Ollie Ladd, swinging away from the bar, came several ponderous strides toward him.

Ollie had been drinking. He had been riding the bottle pretty heavily ever since Kline Hyatt had stripped the deputy's badge and its authority from him. There was turgid flush all through his broad, dark cheeks and his eyes held a sodden, fixed, animal-like glare. Now his lips pulled loosely and he cursed Burke, laying on him the unforgivable epithet.

For a man whose normal movement was paced and solid and deliberate, Burke acted with explosive swiftness. He slithered forward and rolled his heavy, rawboned shoulders behind a driving fist. The impact of the blow was a meaty thud, and it sealed off Ollie Ladd's obscene mouthings as though he'd been struck dead. It sent the hulking ex-deputy reeling back a pace, where he wavered, ponderous and half stunned. Burke moved in and hit him again, hit him twice, tipping Ollie's head back with a driving left, then clubbing a winging right to that open jaw. Ollie fell against the bar, teetered a moment, then went heavily down.

Rubbing the knuckles of his right hand up and down across the palm of his left, Burke eyed Ollie's sprawled figure through a moment of sober silence. Then his head came up and he again eyed Meade Bastian coldly.

"You heard me, Bastian. Stay away from me and mine—and don't try and cross our land!"

With this, Burke turned and paced to the door, Duke Royale stepping aside to let him pass. A stirring movement by some of the combine men set the muzzle of Cam Reeves' shotgun to swinging in a steady arc which covered the room with its threat. The double snick of the hammers as Cam brought them to full cock, made small, but ominous echoes.

"Now there you have it," drawled Cam to Duke Royale. "The reason I brought this gun in here. And can you imagine what it would be like, should I cut loose both barrels?"

There was no answer, and with Burke already safely in the street and a vigilant Gil Yeager at his shoulder, Cam backed through the door and let it swing shut again.

Behind them lay a stunned and baffled room. Again there was a long moment of silence. Then Meade Bastian began beating his fist again and again on the bar, emphasizing a low, bitter monotone of cursing.

Duke Royale turned and moved back through the room, paying no attention at all to Ollie Ladd, now beginning to mumble and stir. Passing Bastian, Royale jerked his arm, and Bastian followed into the back room of the place. Duke Royale slammed shut the door and turned on Bastian savagely.

"Well, that's another deal we lost. This sort of thing keeps on, we'll lose the whole damn game. First there was just Yeager, and we agreed on a finish for him. But we were slow getting around to it. So he got the jump on us, with Trezevant and Mims helping. Now he's got Benedict and Reeves on his side, too. There could be somebody else, tomorrow. We got to do something, and do it quick!"

Bastian flared back at him. "You think I like it this way? Tomorrow I'll—"

"Tomorrow—hell!" cut in Royale. "Tonight, God damn it! Tonight and no later!"

Black and bitter eyes and flaring, pale gray ones met and held. Meade Bastian nodded.

"All right. Tonight it is."

In the barroom, after several tries, Ollie Ladd stumbled erect and leaned against the bar. He spat crimson from mashed lips and called for whiskey.

12.

THE TRAIL RAN out of the upper reaches of Summit Prairie, climbing through timbered country to the gap between the extreme northern limits of the Seminoles and the Redstone Hills, thereafter dropping into a vast stretch of wild country where it converged with several other trails leading in and out of Malvern's Corner.

Here a lone two-storied building lifted above a rickety stable, a couple of sprawling corrals and several sheds. All were raw-boarded, bleached and uncared for to tawdriness. The lower part of the building comprised a combination saloon and store of sorts, while the upper story was made up of several small, cheerless, scantily furnished rooms strung along either side of a narrow hall, where men might sleep.

The place was remote and hard-shelled and when Sheriff

Kline Hyatt rode up to it through the long running shadows of late afternoon, he glimpsed movement of men slipping from sight past the stable and he knew that other eyes were doubtless watching from the blurred windows of the main building. It was that kind of a layout, furtive and suspicious.

Hyatt pulled in before the building, dismounted with slow care and limped inside. He had been all day in the saddle and was thoroughly whipped with weariness. Pausing for a moment at the door to adjust to the gloom, he caught the stirring of the man behind the short bar at the far end of the room. He moved up, leaned against this and let out a gusty sigh.

"You got any liquor worth a damn, Nick, trot it out. Time was when my saddle and me, we got along fine together. But no more. The damn thing's changed into an instrument of torture."

Nick Malvern put bottle and glass on the bar. He was a tall man, lath thin, completely bald and with small, gimlet-sharp eyes pinched in on either side of a great hungry beak of a nose.

"Ain't the saddle that's changed, Hyatt. It's you. Too much office chair. You don't get out this way very often."

Hyatt, pouring himself a stiff jolt, downed it in one long gulp, twisting his lips and shuddering as the raw liquor hit bottom. He wiped his lips with the back of his hand, nodding.

"Damn near a year, Nick." He poured another drink, let it stand before him. A short silence fell, Nick Malvern going through the motions of wiping down the bar with a grimy, thread-bare towel. Hyatt got out a cigar, lit it and drew deep with relish. He sighed a second time. "Now I begin to live again."

Still Nick Malvern said nothing, and Hyatt rolled his cigar across his lips to hide the faint, sardonic smile which touched there. Malvern was suspicious, wary as a hunted wolf. Hyatt took his cigar from his mouth, looked at the glowing tip of it, then put his glance solidly on the man in front of him.

"You're guessing, Nick—and guessing right. I sure as hell

didn't make the ride clear out here just for the fun of it. I'm looking for information."

Nick Malvern shook his egg-bare head. "I don't know a thing, Hyatt. Nothin' ever happens here. Them that come by, I don't bother, and they don't bother me. I sell them a little liquor, a few groceries, maybe. They're here, then they're gone. Nine times out of ten I never see them again. So, how could I know anything about anybody?"

"Sure, sure," murmured Hyatt, a subtle note of scoffing in his words. "But maybe you can jog your memory."

"I got the poorest memory in the world," Malvern said.

Abruptly a stern authority flowed out of Hyatt, and his tone sharpened.

"Men like you, Nick, are all alike. You all come up with the same damn answers in the same damn way. You don't know anything, you don't hear anything, you don't see anything. In short, according to you, you go through life deaf, dumb, blind and helpless. Well, I quit believing that sort of guff a long time ago. You like your setup here?"

"It's a living," Malvern answered sullenly.

"And you'd like to stay?"

"Like to—and intend to!" A thread of defiance came into Malvern's words.

"Don't put your hopes on it," Hyatt said. "That is unless your memory improves. You see, Nick, it's like this. In a bottom drawer of my desk, along with a number of others like it, there's a reward dodger concerning one Tulsa Slim. You know, it's amazing how exact the description fits you. The crime itself ain't much, though a lot of men have been hung for the same thing. A little argument over the true ownership of a horse. I guess the horse didn't amount to much either, for the reward is almost an insult. Just two hundred dollars, that's all. Hardly worth bothering with—unless—" Hyatt turned up his hands and shrugged. "How's your memory coming?"

"Better," said Nick Malvern resignedly.

"Sure," said Hyatt soothingly. "I knew it would. You know, Nick, I'm not like some who are so self-righteous they'd hound a man down on any excuse, just to show their author-ity. Way I see it is that if a man has made a mistake—not too serious a mistake, you understand—and has learned his lesson, and from then on behaves himself pretty well, then there's no sense in beatin' him over the head and wasting good time and money trying to put him over the road. You and me, we can get along together. Nick, what do you know about the killing of Cress Lucas?"

"Cress Lucas! I thought that was all settled in court a year ago. You should know a lot more about it than me. You had a feller named Yeager behind bars for it."

"I know I did," Hyatt said bruskly. "But Yeager had nothing to do with it, which has since been proven."

Nick Malvern stared at Hyatt fixedly. "You've changed, haven't you?"

"Yes," Hyatt said evenly, "I've changed. And I'm ready to change a lot of things if I have to. So now, with the fable of Yeager's guilt tossed out, let's get on toward the truth." Hyatt's tone crisped up as he added, "I know how it is in a place like this. Men drift in and out. They're for the most part anything but our best citizens. Maybe they don't talk much, they do talk some. A word here—a word there. Pretty soon those words connect and make sense. A man like you, behind a bar, he's bound to pick up a lot of information about this and that. Well?"

"I hear a little," admitted Nick Malvern cautiously. "Maybe not the direct facts, but rumors." He broke off to again stare at Hyatt in that fixed, wondering manner. "You really mean you got no idea at all who killed Lucas?"

"God damn it!" exploded Hyatt irritably. "Of course not! If I did would I half cripple myself riding clear out here to ask questions of you? You know something. What is it?"

Malvern began carefully mopping down the bar again.

"Hyatt, I'm giving this to you straight. I know only what I've heard, and it's second or third hand, so you can do your own figgering on what it's really worth. Anyhow, here it is. There's a feller named Offerman—Tate Offerman—who used to ride for that big land and cattle combine down on the prairie. Whether he still does or not, I wouldn't know. Last I heard of him he was holding down a line camp for the combine somewhere over in the Redstone Hills. Now if you can locate him and get him to talk, then, according to rumor, he can tell you plenty about the Cress Lucas killing; not what he heard, but what he actually saw. There you have it. And," Nick Malvern ended with a stubborn finality, "that's all I know and all I'll say, regardless of what you do or don't do to me!"

"For a man who had a temporary lapse of memory, that's pretty good," Hyatt said, drily amiable again. "When I get back to the office I'll tear up that Tulsa Slim dodger. Now let's have a drink together. After which I'll be interested in something to eat and a bed. I'll spend the night with you, Nick."

"Thanks," said Nick Malvern, setting another glass on the bar and reaching for the bottle. "Thanks, I will have that drink. And by God, Hyatt—you sure have changed!"

Tate Offerman was a skinny little man; a bleached and faded little man with a cigarette cough, who liked the lonely, solitary job of a line camp rider. In fact, he had spent a considerable portion of his adult life seeking isolation and anonymity. Because, years before, when one time fired with the recklessness and false courage engendered by an overload of whiskey, he'd committed a minor crime, and had been fleeing from it ever since.

And so he lived, in a mean little line camp, apart from his fellow men and apart from, for him, the great betrayer. Whiskey. Away from it he was a quiet, reticent man, frugal of words. But with only a minor amount of it burning under his belt, his size, in proportion to the world about him, changed magically. He grew large, it grew small. He grew confident, bold. Reticence left him. He talked, he even bragged.

Like the time a traveling rider had stopped by and had

a meal with him. The rider had a pint in his pocket. Between them they killed it, and Tate Offerman, expanding, had boasted of something he had seen. The other rider, a fiddle-foot just passing through, had a day or two later drifted in at Malvern's Corner, and there, making idle talk over Nick Malvern's bar, had related what Tate Offerman had told him. And so, through this somewhat devious and circuitous route had the word reached Sheriff Kline Hyatt and caused him to come riding up to the camp in the Redstones on the afternoon of still another day, there to sit his saddle wearily while looking down at Tate Offerman.

The moment Offerman glimpsed Hyatt's star, all his old fears of the law came back and he was swiftly a harried shrunken little soul. Hyatt was shrewd enough to recognize this fact and, also, shrewd enough to hazard a fairly accurate guess as to the cause of it. So he predicated his manner and attitude accordingly. He was bruskly official.

"You're Tate Offerman?"

Offerman nodded, shrinking a little more.

"I'm seeking information," Hyatt said. "I was told you could furnish me with what I'm after."

"Depends," Offerman said meekly. "I'll do what I can, Sheriff."

"I understand," Hyatt said, holding this faded little man with stern glance, "that you can tell me who killed Cress Lucas. That you saw it happen. Is that so?"

In one way Tate Offerman knew a great relief, in another he was frightened. This man was not digging into his, Tate Offerman's, deep past, but was asking about something as recent as a year previous. At the same time there was never any telling what might happen to an informant. Damn the whiskey and its tongue-loosening propensities!

Inasmuch as Offerman's life-long instinct had always been to dodge or evade, he made a clumsy attempt at it now.

"Who," he demanded, his voice taking on a note of shrill-ness, "said I knew anything about the Cress Lucas shooting? I never had anything to do with it."

"And I never said you did," probed Hyatt remorselessly. "But you saw it happen. That's true, isn't it?"

Tate Offerman just couldn't get away from the demanding impact of Kline Hyatt's words and boring glance. All resistance ran out of him. He gulped and nodded.

"Yeah, I saw it happen. And—and if you don't mind my sayin' so, Sheriff, I can't understand how you could help knowin' all about who did it, right from the first."

Kline Hyatt's eyes pinched down, and bleakness ran all through him. For here, in effect, was the same kind of wonder and incredulity he'd found in Nick Malvern—an inability to really believe he was as much in the dark as he claimed. It was a disturbing thing. Had he been completely blind to something that had been right before him?

True, he hadn't delved too deeply into the affair at the time of its happening. Brick Rand had found the body of Cress Lucas, had sworn to the complaint. Judge Elias Blackmur had issued the murder warrant. And he, Kline Hyatt, together with his then deputy, Ollie Ladd, had made the arrest.

The fact that the charge against Gil Yeager had been based on the thinnest kind of circumstantial evidence, was quite obvious, but at the time, he, Kline Hyatt had chosen to ignore this fact. Technically, his attitude had been within the exact limits of his authority and office. Morally, he had been vastly negligent, and he squirmed now in thinking of it, under the whip of his reawakened conscience.

But what was this thing he had been so blind to?

"Strange as it may seem to you, Offerman," he said tersely, "I don't know who did it, and I've no idea who did it. So—you tell me!"

Tate Offerman licked his lips. "You won't get mad at me, Sheriff? You won't feel I'm slandering—you and your office?"

"Mad at you—for slandering me! Man, just what the hell are you driving at?"

"Why," Offerman said, "it's like this, Sheriff. The man who killed Cress Lucas was your own deputy, Ollie Ladd!"

Kline Hyatt reared high in his saddle. "Ollie Ladd? You're lying!"

"You see," shrugged Tate Offerman dismally. "I knew you'd get your mad up. But I'm telling the truth, so help me! Ollie Ladd killed Cress Lucas. He shot Lucas in the back. I know he did because I saw him do it. Yes, sir—Ollie Ladd killed Cress Lucas!"

In his emphasis, Tate Offerman met Kline Hyatt's grim stare unwaveringly, and Hyatt knew bleak conviction that he was indeed hearing the truth. So, while he tried to get this thing into proper perspective, he urged Offerman to go on.

"All right. You're not lying. Tell me exactly what you saw, and how you happened to see it."

Blinking as he recollected, Tate Offerman told it slowly and carefully.

"Brick Rand had been bunchin' considerable Sixty-six stuff toward the lower end of the lake. At the time I wondered why and found out later when he moved the cattle around to Lazy Y range on the east side. To hold the stock from driftin', he had me ridin' south line.

"Well, it was a pretty hot day and I headed into the shade of that clump of timber above Burnt Corral to rest my saddle and have a smoke. I'm there maybe twenty minutes when here comes Cress Lucas and Ollie Ladd ridin' up the town trail. They seemed friendly enough, talkin' back and forth and such. Right by Burnt Corral they stop and chin some more. Then they move to split up, Lucas comin' on along the trail, while Ollie Ladd made like to turn back. But Ollie, he's watchin' over his shoulder, and when he sees Lucas ain't lookin', he throws his gun and shoots Lucas in the back, just as deliberate and cold-blooded as hell. Then he lights a shuck outa there."

Tate Offerman paused, passed a hand across his eyes as if he'd wipe away something he wished fervently he'd never seen.

"That's it," he went on finally. "That's it, exactly! At first I had the feelin' I'd been seein' things. I remember I closed my eyes, almost certain that when I opened them again I'd find I'd imagined it all. My luck wasn't that good. When I took a second look, there was Cress Lucas down in the trail, with his horse fiddlin' around, spooked and uneasy. And there was Ollie Ladd, dustin' it off in the direction of town."

"What did you do then?" pressed Hyatt.

"I got outa there," Offerman said. "I got back to the cattle and stayed with them."

"Didn't you go see if perhaps Lucas was still alive?"

Offerman shook his head. "He was dead, and I knew it."

"Did you report what you had seen to anyone?"

Again Offerman shook his head.

"Why didn't you?"

Beginning to sweat, Offerman swallowed thickly. "It was none of my business. For all I knew, mebbe Ollie Ladd—him bein' a lawman—had good reason to gun Lucas. Besides—"

"Besides—what?"

"There was no point in me gettin' myself in a mess," Offerman defended desperately. "You know what I mean, Sheriff—mebbe bein' dragged into a court to answer questions and all that sort of thing."

"Why should you be afraid of a few questions?" Hyatt asked. "You had done nothing to worry about."

"Mebbe not," argued Offerman weakly, "but a man never knows what such might lead to. Me, I've found you get along best in this world if you mind your own business."

Kline Hyatt considered this colorless, cringing little man grimly, his thoughts already reaching elsewhere. There was nothing more to be gained here. He stirred in his saddle, lifted the reins.

"All right, Offerman. What you just told me remains between the two of us. You stay here. Should you try and sneak out of the country I'll follow you clear past hell and drag you back by the scruff of the neck. Then you will find things rough!"

Offerman bobbed his head quickly. "I'll be right here any time you want me, Sheriff."

"Good enough."

Kline Hyatt considered the slant of the afternoon sunlight through the timber and judged he'd hit town by dark. He headed that way, his thoughts somber and seeking.

With full dark, air began a movement from the south-east, and by the time Gil Yeager started on his nightly patrol along the lift of land above Rubicon Creek it was a full-bodied wind that was driving down past Sheridan Peak and bustling the length and breadth of Summit Prairie. In it there was chill and the suggestion of wetness to come, and, as Yeager loosed the tie strings about his rolled up coat behind the saddle cantle and donned the .garment, a high mist, racing before the drive of the wind, was first shrinking and dimming the stars, then blotting them out entirely.

Dismounted, and with reins trailing across a shoulder, Yeager hunkered stoically on his heels. Beside him, his horse swung its rump to the wind. Over on the lake the boisterous air was whipping the relatively shallow water to roughness, stirring up the bird life there, setting it awing and restless, and thinly crying through the night.

In the light of day and the depths of dark, mused Yeager, wind was a thing of two faces. An invisible thing in itself by day, yet its effect was plain to the eye. Tossing timber, flying twigs and leaves, miles of open grass bending and flattening before it, small growth writhing and twisting, and lake waters uneasy, whipped to turbulence and frothed with mud-stained foam. All these things gave a daylight wind a substance a man could identify and understand.

In the dark, however, the effect was greatly different. Now the wind was a disembodied voice, shouting across the world. At its peak the tone was shrill and penetrating, then, during a lull, falling to a faint and wistful sighing. But always it was a definite presence, pressing against a man, forever digging and tugging at him with prying, persistent fingers. While on it rode all of man's oldest most primitive fears and superstitions, for it cried aloud of space beyond measure, of eternity and of time's endless limits, and of man's brief walk across the earth and of his minuscule insignificance. . . .

Hunching his shoulders higher, Yeager swung around on his heels and put his back to the wind. Thus sheltering his hands, he spun up a cigarette by feel and got it alight. After which, he turned his thoughts to the happenings of the day.

It had had its moments, all right. There had been his all too brief opportunity to see and talk to Laurie Benedict over at Long B earlier in the day, she slim and poised and contained, in her dress of mourning, he increasingly aware of the reawakening of all the old fervor and sentiment for this girl. Then there had been the quiet, sober interval while old Dave Benedict was laid to his last rest. Finally, there came the harsh, explosive moment when Burke Benedict stood in the Golden Horn and voiced his defiance to Meade Bastian, and followed this by clubbing Ollie Ladd's surly massiveness into senseless subjection.

Recollection of this warmed Yeager. Because it fully substantiated Burke's explanation as to the reason for his past apparent friendliness with Bastian and the combine, while at the same time bringing this condition to a definite end. And it stamped Burke as a savage and competent fighter when fully aroused. Which was so often the way such things turned out. It was the sober, quiet man who carried no chip on his shoulder who was the one to fear when he did break loose and go on a rampage.

When telling of it that evening at supper, Yeager got three different reactions. Jed Mims complained bitterly that if he'd been allowed to go along to town instead of having to spend the day just hanging around the ranch staring at an empty world, he'd have seen Ollie Ladd get his needings, all of which he'd have enjoyed.

Alec Trezevant, listening in silence, had frowned and admitted gruffly it had considerably straightened out his thinking on Burke Benedict.

But it was Anita Trezevant's reaction that interested Yeager most. She had gone very still, while a soft glow came into her dark eyes, and her expressive lips showed a faint, sweet, possessive smiling. And when she began cleaning up the dishes there was a new eagerness in her movements.

As the night hours moved and deepened, the wind held on, if anything growing, rather than diminishing in power. The stars blanked out completely and the darkness became stygian. Several times Yeager went into his saddle and sent his horse casting back and forth along Rubicon Creek, once crossing this and riding south a couple of miles into the wind. Close to midnight a flurry of rain fell, but dwindled off as Yeager rode back to headquarters. He unsaddled and corraled his horse, then stole into the bunkhouse with extra care, deciding not to bother Alec Trezevant for late guard. But old Alec was already awake, and when Yeager came in, he got up and began getting dressed.

"Go on back to bed, Alec," directed Yeager. "It's a wild night out, and getting worse. It's already rained a little, and by the feel of things is due to storm plenty before daylight. It's no kind of night for anybody to prowl in, and there's no sense in you punishing yourself."

"Hell—it won't be the first stormy night I've been out in," growled old Alec as he pulled on his boots. "When I reach the point where a little wind and rain keeps me indoors, then I'll crawl off in a corner out of everybody's way. And you're wrong on the other point, Gil. Now if I was aiming to pull a surprise attack this is just the kind of night I'd want for it, figuring the other feller would be thinking just like you are now. No, sir—either we guard all the time, or there's no sense in guarding at all. Don't worry about me. I'll do all right."

There was a yellow oil-skin slicker hanging on a nail beside the door and Alec Trezevant took this with him as he went out.

In his bunk, Yeager propped on one elbow while he finished a final cigarette. Then he dropped back, pulled the blankets about him and was soon asleep.

He had no idea how long he had slept before the sound

came down the night to break through the barrier of sleep and awaken him. He lay quiet, wondering. It was black dark and the wind was huffing and puffing and rumbling about the corners of the bunkhouse. Also there was rain, pounding on the roof, splashing heavily down from the eaves, while the wet breath of it came misting through an open window.

This, the wind and the rain, Yeager thought, was what had awakened him. He turned over and reached again for sleep.

But now once more there was the sound, one there was no mistaking, riding in on the wind from the south. Way out there a rifle had snarled, and now, quickly, a third flat, hard report cut through the voice of the storm.

Yeager surged from his blankets.

"Jed!" he called sharply. "Jed!"

Jed was already reaching for his boots. "I heard that one, Gil. Alec's in trouble out there!"

13.

THEY CAUGHT UP guns and broke from inner to outer dark, and where the one had been dry and warm, the other was a torment of chill wind and drenching rain. It had been Gil Yeager's first thought that he and Jed must catch and saddle and get out there where Alec Trezevant held lonely post in this black and stormy world, but now, carried on the wind was the pound of speeding hoofs, and then it was a rider racing in from the south.

"Alec!" yelled Yeager, hoping.

"Right!" came the harsh, tight answer. "They're close behind, and hell bent. Don't hold back, Gil—because they won't. This is it!"

"You take the ranchhouse, Alec, and Jed the east side. I'll hang on here."

They swung away and now he was alone, with the rain whipping his face and the wind buffeting him, and he wondered what a man could do of any account in a dark like this, when hearing was of little use and sight none at all. Yet, as he waited, senses straining, eyes staring, he found that a man's faculties could attune surprisingly to emergency; that sound could reach him after all, and that a darkness which had seemed utter, was not.

From a little way out there came the mutter of hoofs, and off to his left the rails and posts of corral fence sprouted into vague tracery. He moved over beside the fence, crouching slightly, and, even with Alec Trezevant's warning sharp in his mind, knew a hesitancy at making this an outright thing. So, when night brought further suggestion of movement, he lifted his warning call.

"Far enough, out there—far enough!"

There could be no mistaking the mood of the answer he got. Several guns opened up, shooting at the sound of his call, their combined reports a pounding, sullen threat in the dark. Speeding lead made impact all about him, a thick and soggy sound where it struck wet earth, but sharper and more distinct when against corral post or rail.

Something plucked at Yeager's sleeve and a scorching line streaked across his left forearm. It was as if, for a fractional second, a thread of live fire had touched. But it wasn't fire, he realized bleakly. That touch had been a bullet, meant for his heart.

He dropped to one knee and swung the lever of his rifle rapidly, flailing the dark three times, shooting at those winking gun flashes. He heard a man's stricken cry, and then, rocketing out of the gloom came a riderless horse, spooked and running wild. The animal smashed into the corral fence not ten yards from where Yeager crouched, bounced off and raced away.

Someone yelled, "Circle right and left! Get around—get around!"

Yeager shot at the sound of the voice, and this brought

another flurry of answering fire. After which there was a breaking rush away on either hand.

Over at the ranchhouse, Alec Trezevant's heavy rifle struck up a measured rumble, and there was the wink and crash of shooting in return. Until now, Yeager had moved and acted pretty much in a mechanical way, his actions instinctive and without any greatly considered feeling. But now he knew a sudden, convulsing rage. For Anita Trezevant was in that ranchhouse, and the damned combine guns were shooting that way. He started to move to Alec's support, but stopped abruptly as two riders came straight in on him at a furious pace. He had no time to shoot, only enough to throw himself headlong to one side and so avoid being ridden down. Then the two were past and whirling to a stop somewhere among the ranch buildings behind him. Yeager picked himself out of the mud and shouted a warning to Jed Mims.

"Watch in back of you, Jed—in back of you!"

Over east a rattle of outside shots sounded, followed by several evenly spaced more solid ones closer at hand, which, Yeager knew, came from Jed's carbine. But Jed made no other answer, so there was no way to tell if he'd heard that shouted warning. There was, Yeager decided, but one thing to do. He must drop back among the ranch buildings, gambling that an all-out frontal rush would be hesitant in developing. And those two riders who had got by must be located and rooted out, for they were the immediate danger.

As he moved cautiously back he tried to figure the intent of the enemy two. Which way would they be liable to strike, at the ranchhouse, at Jed—at himself? He shook his head. It was of little use. Any guess would be just that, and no more.

The drumming of the wind against a wall told him he was close to the saddle shed, with bunkhouse and cookshack beyond, and with the swing of the corral fence off to the east, leading to barn and feed sheds. A jungle of dark buildings, among which prowled two of the enemy.

Yeager got his shoulders against the end of the saddle shed and sidled past a corner of it. Immediately the acrid odor of wet, steamy horseflesh struck his nostrils. Here, almost within reach of his hand, were the mounts of the two riders. But where were the latter?

He went still, listening, probing the dark as best he could. There could be, he realized, no mistake in this, for it had become a starkly deadly game. Where the hovering danger—where—?

Over east by the barn, faint through the rustle of the storm, came a man's startled challenge, followed closely by two flatly thudding revolver shots. On the heels of these a rifle crashed—once. After which silence held for a space until Alec Trezevant's old buffalo Sharps again rumbled at the ranchhouse.

Yeager wanted to call again to Jed Mims, to get answer from him, but knew this wouldn't do. For wherever the two skulkers were, they'd have to return for their horses. But should he chance waiting for them where he was, or should he go looking for them? Even as he pondered this, it was answered for him.

A man charged up through the dark, panting heavily, and cursing in the dull, mechanical way that told of uncertainty and mounting fear. The horses wheeled away at this headlong approach and the man's cursing pitched higher as he directed it at the uneasy animals. Sensing, rather than actually seeing the position of the fellow, Yeager threw a sharp word at him.

"You—!"

The man whirled, gasping audibly, and drove a blind shot which battered the shed wall high and to one side of Yeager. With that gun flash to guide its pointing, Yeager's rifle now smashed back its answer, and it belted a strangled groan and two choked words from a mortally stricken target.

"Oh—God—!"

The two horses, thoroughly spooked now by the flaring guns so close to them, plunged off, dragging grounded reins. Yeager levered another cartridge home in his rifle and waited —and waited.

There was no sound now except for the wail of the wind about the corners of buildings, and the splash of rain sheeting down from gorged eaves. Shooting had stopped everywhere. But presently a long shout came in from the outer dark.

"Starker—Mitch Starker! Hey—Mitch—answer up!"

There was no answer, and the same call came in again. Still no answer, and then there was no further calling, nor shooting, and slowly the conviction came to Yeager that for this night at least, assault was done.

Or was it night? Despite the murk of the storm a vague grayness was seeping over the world and all around objects were taking on form and fiber. Here abruptly, was the breaking dawn.

Yonder was the bunkhouse and against the dark mass of this there was shifting movement by the two horses that had spooked that way. Just a few steps away there was a huddle of dark shadow against the still darker earth, and Yeager moved slowly up to it. The huddle was a man, doubled and still. Yeager dropped to one knee, peered closely. The man was a stranger and he was dead.

Yeager came back slowly to his feet, his thoughts tired and somber. In the final dark moment before dawn's breaking, he and this man had faced each other, total strangers, and traded shots. Now the man lay dead, another sacrifice to the land and cattle greed of others.

Yeager shook himself. Here was neither time or place for soft or sentimental thinking. This was still a world of stark and brutal realities, and a man, if he were to survive, had to gear his every move to meet them. Like that call for Mitch Starker, which Starker had not answered. Why hadn't he answered—and what about him? And of Jed Mims, who had not answered to a shout either?

A dismal fear gusted through Yeager and he headed out past a feed shed toward the barn, where that last flurry of close at hand shooting had taken place. Thirty feet from the barn he nearly stumbled over Mitch Starker. He knew at a

143

glance that it was Starker, even though the burly figure lay sprawled face down and shrunken in death.

Yeager's concern did not linger long on the combine bully boy, but reached on to where Jed Mims was sagged down in a sitting position, shoulders propped against the barn.

Yeager ran to him, caught at him. "Jed—Jed, were you hit? How bad—?"

Jed's answer to Yeager's words and touch was to topple over and lie loose and still. There was a bullet hole through the base of Jed's throat.

Subsequent action was almost automatic with Yeager. Just past the corner of the barn there was an open door. and through this, where he might be out of the storm, Yeager half carried, half dragged Jed Mims' lifeless figure. Then he tramped over to the ranchhouse, where now a lamp was burning, a pale yellow eye in the kitchen window.

"Yeager coming in," he said harshly, as he opened the kitchen door.

He stepped in and went abruptly still. Alec Trezevant sat on one chair, with his right leg propped up on another. Anita Trezevant had just scissored away the leg of the mud- and blood-stained jeans, exposing an angry looking wound a little above the knee. Old Alec, his face drawn and tight, spoke past pain-gritted teeth.

"Their last damn shot. I was at a window. The slug hit just below that, came through and knocked this leg out from under me. Missed the bone, but it still ain't doing me any good. They're gone though, Gil. They had enough, this time."

"Yes," said Yeager, in a harsh, numbed way. "Enough. But we've had—too much."

Alec's head jerked up. "What do you mean? Jed—he's hurt?"

"He's dead," Yeager said tonelessly.

Anita Trezevant gave a tragic little cry, while a shadow of pain in no way related to his injured leg, brushed across old Alec's face.

"How did it happen?"

"Mitch Starker and another combine hand made a rush and got in close. They tangled with Jed. One of them got him, but he got Mitch Starker. I took care of the other one."

"And all on the head of Meade Bastian," growled Alec bitterly.

"And mine," Yeager said bleakly. "I dragged Jed and you in on a fight that should have been all my own. Yeah, Jed's dead because I didn't go it alone. And—"

"Hell with that kind of talk," broke in Alec gruffly. "Jed knew what he was doing. So did I. You didn't sell us any pig in a poke. You were set to stage a fight for the rights of every decent rancher, past and present, on Summit Prairie. Jed and me, we figgered it was our fight, too, so we sat into it. So don't go around banging your head against the wall and blaming yourself."

Yeager shook himself and met Anita Trezevant's eyes. Soft, dark eyes, tear-misted, now. She spoke gently.

"Dad's right, Gil. It's not your fault. These—these things just happen."

He moved over beside her. "I'll help you with that leg. Then we're clearing out of here. They've gone for now, but they'll be back."

"Tie up the leg, prop me at a window and give me my old Sharps gun," Alec growled. "Then it'll take a damned shifty man to get by."

"No!" Yeager said. "The full effect of that leg hasn't begun to hit, yet. When it does, you'll forget all about sitting at a window doing anything. You'll be flat on your back, yelling for help. All right, Anita."

Between them they washed the wound and got a bandage on it. By the time they had finished, Alec was slumped in his chair, face gray and sweating.

"You're right," he said between set teeth. "Afraid I couldn't hold that old Sharps very steady just now."

"I'll go after Doc Parris, soon as I get you two over to the Long B," Yeager said.

Anita exclaimed softly. "The Long B! Have we the right? Would we be welcome, Gil? I wouldn't want—"

"You'll be welcome," Yeager said. "There's always been a welcome waiting for you and Alec at Long B."

"But what if Meade Bastian and his crowd follow?"

"They won't," assured Yeager. "I'm the one Bastian wants. I'll get the horses ready."

Leaving the house he moved into full daylight. The wind had dropped and the rain lessened, and over east along the Seminoles the cloud masses were thinning and lifting.

But there was no thinning or lifting of the gray and bitter mood which held Yeager. His face was stony, his thoughts cold and accusing. Despite the reassurance which Alec and Anita had just tried to give him, he saw it as his fault that right now Jed Mims lay dead over in the barn yonder, and that Alec Trezevant was writhing and sweating with the agony of a bullet-slashed leg.

For no other real consideration than friendship, these two men had stood beside him against heavy odds, to aid him and his interests. And how useless their sacrifice!

Well, there was one real and permanent solution to this thing, a solution he should have applied in the very beginning. To kill a snake you cut off the head, not the tail. Yes, that had been the initial answer and it was the answer now. So be it . . . !

Fresh from a shave, and then in the back bath room of George Clyte's barber shop, a hot scrubbing and change of clothes, Sheriff Kline Hyatt had supper at the Elite, then headed for the Summit House Hotel. At the hotel bar he bought some cigars from Bill Spelle, and, after lighting one, asked his question.

"Brick Rand still with you, Bill?"

"Yeah," answered Spelle. "And," added the hotel owner bluntly, "I wish he wasn't. I never did like him. Taking care of him is a damn nuisance. He has to be fed soup through a tube. Never saw such a change in a man. When Gil Yeager gave him that going over, he busted more in Rand than just his jaw. He busted Rand's spirit—put the everlasting fear of God into him, what I mean. You know how Rand used to be. Arrogant as hell, so damned sure of himself; heavy with his hands, heavy with his tongue. Well, that's all gone, now. He seems all shrunk up in a funny way, as if all his insides had left him. And his eyes are scared."

"Can he talk yet?"

"Some. Kind of mumbles. Doc Parris has got his face tied up pretty solid. You want to see him?"

Hyatt nodded. "If it's all right with you."

"Help yourself. Room eight."

There was a lamp on the room's small table. It was turned low and the resultant scant light only partly disclosed the face of the man in bed. Even so, Kline Hyatt saw enough to startle him. The lower half of Brick Rand's face was massed with bandage, but above this his eyes were sunken, feverishly bright and staring in a strange, wild way.

At a glance, Kline Hyatt understood what Bill Spelle meant. As the result of a savage physical beating, this man in the bed had lost all former confidence and belief in himself. Right now Brick Rand was an unstable shadow fleeing from mental terror.

"Brick," said Hyatt, "I'm looking for information and I'm pretty sure you can give it to me. I'm looking for the name of the man who killed Cress Lucas."

Brick Rand gave a start and his staring glance shifted. Muffled words came from between the folds of bandage.

"Yeager killed Lucas."

Hyatt rolled his cigar across his lips. "Won't do, Brick," he countered, his tone hardening. "A dirty deal tried to fasten the killing of Lucas on Gil Yeager, an innocent man. It didn't work out. Yeager never killed him. But you know who did, Brick—and I want the truth. Who did it?"

"Yeager," insisted the man in the bed.

Kline Hyatt sighed. "I was afraid I'd have to get tough with you, Brick. You know damn well that Shad Emmett swore false witness, and that he now gives Yeager a clear alibi. And you know who killed Lucas. Maybe you did, Brick. Which is Judge Carmody's theory. And the more I think on it, the more I think it's a pretty good one. You got an alibi to prove you didn't?"

Brick Rand did not answer, but beneath the blankets he shifted and twisted and a hunted look added to the staring wildness in his eyes.

"There is an old theory, and a sound one," went on Hyatt remorselessly, "that silence—refusal to answer—is an admission of guilt. So I'm arresting you, Brick—for the murder of Cress Lucas. I'll have a bed fixed up for you in the jail, and I'll move you there, first thing in the morning. I can swear Bill Spelle in as deputy to see that you don't sneak off during the night. Of course—" here Hyatt took his cigar from his lips and brushed the ash from it with meticulous care, "of course you could be covering up for someone else. In which case, you're a plain damn fool. Any man who puts his own neck in a noose, trying to cover up for a killer, is a damn fool. What do you think?"

Again Brick Rand shifted and twisted and sweat started at the edge of his carroty thatch. A week ago, Kline Hyatt knew, the Brick Rand of then would have laughed at him and told him to do his damndest and to hell with him. But this was now, and Brick Rand was a vastly different individual than he'd been a week ago. Now he was a man with all arrogance and self-assurance beaten out of him. Now he was a man who lived with a great and haunting fear, and because of that fear the dam broke, suddenly.

"All right—all right," came the mumbled admission. "Yeager didn't kill Lucas. Ollie—Ollie Ladd did."

Kline Hyatt nodded, as though something he had wanted to be absolutely sure of, was now confirmed. He probed on swiftly.

"But by your order, Brick?"

"No, not mine. I was takin' orders, myself. From the Bastians, Meade and Duke."

148

"Ah!" Hyatt murmured. "Then it isn't—Duke Royale. It's Duke Bastian?"

Rand nodded. "Twins, them two. Only their eyes are different. Like sports in a litter."

"I've wondered about that," admitted Hyatt. "They own part of the land and cattle combine?"

"They own all of it. They are the combine."

"And they figured the frame-up on Yeager?"

"That's right," Rand mumbled. "They knew there'd been bad blood between Lucas and Yeager and they figured to get two birds with one shot. Lucas owned the Burnt Corral range, and with him dead, that would be open for easy taking. And with Yeager put over the road for the killing—well—there you have it."

"Yeah," Hyatt murmured sardonically. "Don't we, though. And Ollie Ladd—he was all combine, right from the start?"

"You knew he was," Rand said.

Hyatt nodded slowly, his eyes turning somber. "To a degree, yes. But not quite to that degree." He turned and moved toward the door. Brick Rand came up slightly on one elbow.

"I opened up—I gave you the truth, Hyatt. Don't that earn me a break?"

Across a shoulder, Hyatt considered him. "I don't know, Brick. You'll just have to take your chances. I'm not promising you a damn thing."

Hyatt left, then, returning to the hotel bar, where Bill Spelle was tidying up the bottle shelf.

"Well," demanded the hotel owner, "what do you think?"

"Why," said Hyatt slowly, "mainly I think that by and large, man has a long way to go before becoming as noble as he likes to consider himself."

Bill Spelle blinked. "Now that's a hell of a queer answer."

"Isn't it, though," agreed Hyatt. "But in a lot of ways, it's a hell of a queer world. Good night, Bill—and thanks!"

He stepped out into a night that had become thick, with a buffeting wind stampeding through town and with the

smell of impending rain in the air. He went along to the
Golden Horn and turned in there, seeking. Except for a lone
bartender killing time over a hand of solitaire, the place was
deserted. Of this individual, Hyatt asked:

"Ollie Ladd been around this evening?"

The bartender shook his head.

"Any idea where he'd be?"

"Probably out at combine headquarters, nursing his
wounds."

"Wounds! What do you mean?"

The bartender straightened, whipped the cards together
and began another shuffle.

"Had you been in here right around noon today, you'd
know what I mean. Burke Benedict comes in, stepping
plenty wide for him. He and Meade Bastian have a few
words and it ended up with Benedict telling Meade off—and
good! That fellow Yeager, and Benedict's foreman, Cam
Reeves, they showed up to back Benedict's hand, Reeves
packing a sawed-off shotgun. You might say they sort of spit
in Meade Bastian's eye, too; and in Duke Royale's for that
matter. Anyway, Benedict gets his chest unloaded and then
Ollie Ladd starts cussing out Benedict. Man—you should have
seen the rest!"

"What about the rest?" demanded Hyatt.

"Why," said the bartender, "Burke Benedict proceeded to
knock Ollie hell west and crooked. He sure made a good dog
out of him. Me, I never figured Burke Benedict as being that
tough. He's always been such a quiet, mind-his-own-business
sort. About Ollie—you want to leave a message for him, in
case he should show up?"

"No," said Hyatt slowly, shaking his head as he turned to
leave. "No thanks. What I got for Ollie, I'll deliver myself."

14.

THEY CAME IN at the Long B headquarters as the remnants of last night's storm were breaking and fleeing before the push of a wind that had lessened to a brisk breeze and had swung around so that now it came in from the west across the Redstone Hills. Along the crest of the Seminoles, through gaps in the fast thinning clouds, morning's sun shot long, golden lances of light, and where these touched the prairie it glistened, clean washed and stirring with a fresh vitality.

In the lead, Alec Trezevant rode, his left leg straight and the boot solid in the stirrup. But his wounded right leg, deep padded in a blanket that was wrapped around and around, was a thick, loose-hanging bundle. At his left hand rode his daughter, Anita, ready to offer a supporting arm should her father show signs of weakening in the saddle. But though his face was fine drawn to a dark cragginess, with his eyes pinched down, his lips a thin, set line, and his shoulders hunched, he sat steady in the leather.

Ten yards back came Gil Yeager, and behind him, in a shroud of tarpaulin and face down across the saddle of a led horse, Jed Mims rode. The bitterest task Gil Yeager had known in all his life had been single-handedly getting Jed's body loaded across that saddle. The effect of it still held him and his face was drained and stoic.

As they splashed through the brown, fast-running water of the ditch at the head of the lane and moved on across the interval, Cam Reeves and Burke Benedict showed simultaneously, Burke hurrying from the ranchhouse, Cam coming from the bunkhouse. As these two came up, Yeager explained harshly.

"The combine hit us early this morning. We managed to fight them off, but not until they'd left their mark. They killed Jed Mims and put a slug through Alec's leg. I couldn't leave Alec and Anita there alone, so I brought them here. I told them they'd be welcome, Burke. Are they?"

"Of course," assured Burke swiftly. "Always."

He was looking at Anita Trezevant as he spoke and a little flutter of emotion ran up the soft line of her throat, while something great and wonderful shone in her eyes.

Switching his glance to Alec, Burke said: "We'll put you in Uncle Dave's old room. You'll be handy for looking after, there."

"I don't want to be any damned bother," growled Alec. "The bunkhouse is good enough for me."

"You," said Burke, voice gruff with a mock sternness, "will go where I say and do as I say. Let's get out of that saddle."

Both Cam Reeves and Yeager, who had swung down, moved to help. But Burke was ahead of them. He eased Alec from his horse, lifted him in his big arms and strode into the house with him, Anita following closely, a small satchel in her hand.

Cam Reeves turned to Yeager. "What about Jed?" he asked gravely.

"I'm taking him to town, so that Doc Parris can see to it that he has a decent burial," Yeager said.

"Did you do any good against that combine crowd?"

"Some," Yeager said somberly. "Mitch Starker and one other for certain. There might have been more, out in the dark."

"So it was that bad?"

Yeager nodded. "It was that bad."

"What are you going to do, now?"

"What I should have done in the first place. Cut off the head instead of the tail."

As Cam Reeves blinked, trying to figure this out, a soft, clear call came from the ranchhouse porch.

"Gil! Come here, please."

It was Laurie Benedict, slim and anxious and robed in beauty as a shaft of clean-washed morning sunlight struck up a glow all about her.

He moved up to her slowly, a little stiffly, as though burdened with a spiritual as well as a physical weariness. Standing beside her he looked at her with grave absorption. He spoke as though voicing a thought aloud.

"It's hard to believe that the same world can hold a loveliness such as yours, and at the same time the kind of ugliness that moved through the dark just past, Laurie."

She met his glance mistily, and dropped a hand on his arm.

"You had a very bad night of it, didn't you, Gil? You've had so many bad nights of it, over the past year. And this the worst of all?"

"It was—bad," he nodded.

She asked the same question Cam Reeves had. "What will you do now, Gil?"

Unconsciously his tone hardened. "I'm looking up certain people."

Her feminine intuition was sharp, her wisdom deep. She shivered. "Not now, Gil. Think it over. Stay here with us until you've had time to—"

"No!" The word burst from him harshly. "There'll be no more friends of mine shot up because of me. This I handle alone!"

Her hand tightened on his arm. "Please, Gil. There must be other ways than—than what I know you're thinking of."

He shook his head. "I held with that idea, once. And all it ever got me was more and heavier beatings. So, I know the one answer, now. It comes pretty close to being what Johnny Hock told me the first night of my return. Either I have to leave this prairie for good—or somebody else does. And I don't intend to leave!"

He patted her hand, turned away, tramped back to his horse and went into the saddle.

Cam Reeves, waiting, said, "Hold up until I dress a bronc and I'll ride with you."

"No you won't," Yeager told him. "Understand, I appreciate the thought, but your place is right here on Long B, to help Burke in case Bastian and his crowd go completely savage. That is, before I can get at Bastian."

Fully understanding now what Yeager was about, Cam tried to argue. "Alone, you won't stand a chance. How you going to get at Bastian with his outfit all around him? You'll just get yourself killed, and what good will that do?"

"There's always a time and a place and a way," Yeager said, staring straight ahead, as though already visualizing these three necessary elements. "Also, maybe Bastian's hand isn't as strong as it seems. Maybe some of those combine riders don't like the going when it gets too rough. Last night, outside of Mitch Starker and one other, they didn't appear anxious to get too close. Maybe the idea of dying for forty dollars a month isn't exactly popular with them. Lots of time it isn't, with men of that sort."

"You could be right about the average run of combine hands," Cam Reeves admitted. "But don't ever think the same applies to Meade Bastian and Duke Royale—especially to Duke Royale. There's one who is strictly poison!"

"That may be," Yeager said. "We'll see."

He reined about and away, the horse carrying Jed Mims at lead behind him.

The town of Tuscarora, street puddled, and eaves of buildings still slowly dripping from last night's storm, sluggishly faced the new day, waiting the lift of the sun past Sheridan Peak before coming fully alert and up to its daily activities.

Doc Parris, coat collar turned high against morning's lingering chill, went into the Elite for late breakfast and there met Kline Hyatt. The sheriff, having just finished his meal, was lighting up the first cigar of the day. He was still wearing his belt gun and Doc indicated this with a tip of his head while speaking a little testily, which was his way at times.

"Heard you'd buckled that on. What's the idea—you expecting trouble?"

Hyatt shrugged and switched the subject smoothly. "Nice rain we had."

"Any rain's nice if you're under a roof," Doc said gruffly. "But if somebody had got the epizootic or some other damn thing last night and I'd been called out, I'd have done some tall cussing."

Hyatt smiled thinly. "Yet you'd have gone, just the same. You know, Doc—if you were just half as rough and tough as you like to act, you'd have a rind on you an inch thick. As it is you don't fool anybody, and we kind of like you in these parts."

Doc's answer was a testy grunt, but as he moved on to the table his eyes, under their bushy brows, were twinkling.

Kline Hyatt wheeled out into the street and pausing there, made sober survey of the town. Over opposite, Patch Kelly was opening his store for the day's business, while down at Johnny Hock's establishment two freight outfits were making up, preparing for the long haul out to Gardnerville and way points. The semi-weekly stage, already made up and with Mike Wagner at the reins, came rolling up street, team brisk and eager to go, traces jangling. It would stop at the hotel, pick up the mail and any chance passenger, after which it would head for Mission Grade, drop down the long windings of this and move on into the flat, far-running miles of the lower plains country.

Aside from such small activity the street was empty. For some little time Kline Hyatt stood held in somber thought as he measured the probabilities of the day ahead. Would Ollie Ladd show in town this day or would he have to be searched for? Hyatt's lips twisted in distaste at the thought of having to hit the saddle again, for lingering effects of the two days of riding he'd already put in were still with him in the shape of sore and stiffened muscles. He would, he finally decided, wait until noon or a little after for Ollie to show, and if his man didn't appear by that time, then he'd go looking for him. This decision arrived at, Hyatt tramped along to the courthouse and his office.

Johnny Hock, having seen the stage away, gave some last minute instructions to the skinners of the two freight outfits, and when these had lumbered off, heavy and creaking, made for the Elite, eager for morning coffee and breakfast. He offered greeting to Doc Parris and took place at the table across from him.

They traded idle talk and were on their second cup of coffee when hoofs beat a muffled mutter along the wet street. Shortly a rider came clanking in, a hatchet-faced combine hand by name of Trip Rogers. He had the sunken-eyed, mentally battered look of one who had spent a hard night with no sleep. He ordered a cup of coffee and stood at the counter, gulping it. Then he turned to Doc Parris.

"You're wanted out at headquarters, Doc. One of the boys is jammed up a little."

"What's the matter with him?" Doc demanded.

Trip Rogers hesitated slightly. "He's got a smashed shoulder."

"How did he get it—fall off a horse?"

"No," came the reluctant answer. "He stopped a bullet."

Doc twisted around in his chair, alert and interested. "So-o! How did that happen?"

"I don't know," Rogers answered, going a little sullen and moving to the door. "All I know is I was to find you and send you out to headquarters."

"You're lying, of course," Doc said flatly. "About knowing so little, I mean. Well, if there's a smashed shoulder out there I can promise one certain thing. The owner of it has got himself a peck of trouble ahead." Doc pushed his chair back and stood up. "I may have to bring him in to the office to do a real job on him, so you better hook up a buckboard for me, John. I'll be right along, soon as I get my gear."

Doc paid his score and hurried out. Johnny Hock would

have liked to linger over a third cup, of coffee, but he respected Doc's urgency, so went back to his layout, turning into the wide, shadowy runway of the livery barn, looking for a hostler.

Two saddled horses stood half way along the runway. Across the saddle of one was tied a grimly indicative, tarpaulin wrapped figure. Past the head of the other horse stepped Gil Yeager. He spoke mechanically.

"Hello, John. All right with you if I leave Jed Mims in your harness room until I can locate Doc Parris?"

"Jed Mims!" exclaimed Johnny Hock. "Where—oh—!" He stared at the tarpaulin-covered figure and his tone went muted and shocked. "Good Lord, Gil—don't tell me—!"

"That's it," Yeager cut in. "The combine hit us out at Lazy Y. They killed Jed and crippled Alec Trezevant. You know where Doc Parris is?"

"He'll be right along," Johnny Hock said, recovering a little. "I got to get a rig hooked up for him. A rider out at combine headquarters has got a bullet through his shoulder."

"Good!" said Yeager harshly, beginning to loosen the tie rope that held Jed Mims across his saddle. "Too bad it isn't through his heart. Too bad the whole damn layout ain't in the same fix. They killed Jed, and he was too good a man to die that way. How's for a hand?"

Between them they got Jed Mims laid out on the floor of the harness room. They had just finished with this when Doc Parris came hurrying. Initially as startled as Johnny Hock had been, Doc swore with quiet vehemence as he listened to Yeager's explanation. After which he made grim observation.

"Something like this was bound to happen, of course. It's been in the air ever since the combine started out to overrun the prairie. Such high-handed piracy always ends up in gunsmoke and with dead men on the ground. I don't give a damn how big you are or how rich you are, you can't go around beating the little fellow over the head and get away with it forever. Sooner or later he has taken all he can, and then he starts hitting back and there's hell to pay. And," ended Doc shrewdly, "it's not finished yet, is it?"

"No," Yeager said, "not finished by a hell of a ways. You'll —take care of Jed, Doc? And get out and fix Alec Trezevant's leg up right?"

"I'll head for Long B first of all," promised Doc. "The smashed shoulder at combine headquarters will have to wait."

When Doc rolled away in a buckboard, Yeager turned his two horses over to the hostler and went along with Johnny Hock to the latter's office. Eyeing Yeager keenly, Johnny brought out bottle and glass and poured a stiff three fingers of whiskey.

"Put that away," he advised gruffly. "It'll unlock things for you—take some of the wire out of your insides. When did you eat last?"

"Now that you mention it, last night," Yeager answered. He downed the whiskey, waited a moment, then sighed deeply and reached for his smoking. "You were right, John. I needed that."

"And now you need some food," Johnny said. "While I could stand another cup of coffee myself. Come on."

Crossing to the Elite, Yeager had his look along the street. At the hitch rail of the Golden Horn, two horses now were tied. Johnny Hock paid these no attention, but Yeager marked them keenly and became increasingly bleak and withdrawn as he put his breakfast away, wolfing the hot food before the drive of a sudden and rapacious hunger. Johnny Hock sipped his coffee and tried with gruff, casual words to break through Yeager's mood.

"I know how you feel about old Jed. But that's the way things go, sometimes. It could just as easy been you to stop that slug."

"Maybe," Yeager agreed darkly. "But it was—Jed. And if I'd been a little quicker on the shoot, they'd never have got to him. It's a mistake I won't make again."

Leaving the eating house, Johnny Hock asked: "What's for you now, Gil?"

"Little talk with Kline Hyatt."

"You think he'll side you?"

Yeager shrugged. "We'll see."

He angled away up the street. Frowning, Johnny Hock stared after him, troubled as to Yeager's real intent. Finding no answer to the puzzle, he went slowly back to his office.

Passing the Golden Horn, Yeager had another look at the horses on the rail. One carried a Sixty-six brand, the other, a powerful, close-coupled grullo, wore a patchwork of indecipherable Indian brands. For Yeager's purpose, however, these marked the animal as definitely as might a painted sign.

The reek of fresh cigar smoke along the basement hall of the courthouse indicated Kline Hyatt in his office. When Yeager showed at the door, Hyatt looked up from some paper work, pushed away from his desk and leaned back in his chair, eyeing his visitor keenly.

"You," he said, "are packing a damn mean look this morning. Are you bringing me trouble?"

"Depends," Yeager said briefly. "Sixty-six raided me just before daylight. They killed Jed Mims and crippled Alec Trezevant. They left two of their crew behind that I know of. Mitch Starker and another. Both done for."

However much this word might have startled him, Kline Hyatt showed it only by sitting a little straighter in his chair, and by the gleam in his eye.

"So!" he murmured. "They made the big mistake, eh? I thought they were smarter than that. You want me to go after them, I suppose?"

Yeager shrugged. "That's up to you."

"Which sounds like you might have some ideas of your own—maybe?"

"Maybe."

Hyatt stared straight ahead, rolling his cigar across his lips. "You got any idea if Ollie Ladd was in on the raid?"

"All I'm certain about is Mitch Starker and the other one,

who was a stranger to me," Yeager said. "You ought to know more about Ollie Ladd than me. He was your man."

"Since I took his star away from him I haven't seen him," Hyatt said soberly. "But I've been finding out things about him. If you recall, when I was by the Lazy Y the other morning, I told you I was looking for the man who really did kill Cress Lucas. Well, I've got the answer. Ollie Ladd killed him."

"No!" ejaculated Yeager, truly startled. "You sure?"

"Sure enough," Hyatt nodded. "I got admission of the fact from Brick Rand, as well as the testimony of an eye witness. Ollie did that killing, and now, when I think about it, it figures. But so help me, I never considered it before. Now I'm looking for Ollie. I want him."

"You won't have far to look," Yeager said. "I think he's in the Golden Horn right now."

Hyatt came to his feet. "You saw him there?"

"No, I didn't see him. But that grullo bronc of his is tied out front."

"Then he must have ridden in since I had my last look down that way," Hyatt said. "I've been keeping watch, hoping he'd hit town."

So saying, Hyatt settled his gun belt a little more securely about his lank middle and moved out into the hall. Yeager fell into step with him. When they reached the street, Hyatt paused and fixed a narrow glance on Yeager.

"Where do you think you're going?"

"Why," Yeager murmured, meeting the glance, "I figure to trail along with you."

"Maybe I don't want you along."

"Why not?"

"Because," said Hyatt carefully, "if I know Ollie Ladd's makeup—and I think I do—he'll never submit to peaceful arrest. So, when I brace him, it could turn rough."

"And that will be all right with me," Yeager said. "For it was plenty rough out at Lazy Y this morning, and it's left me feeling pretty rough, myself. Ollie Ladd won't be alone in that dive. There's at least one other combine man with him. Which could be Mister Meade Bastian. And there could always be Duke Royale, too. In which case, I want to see that sweet brotherly pair just as bad as you want to see Ollie Ladd. Now, do I go into the Golden Horn with you—or do I go in by myself?"

For a little time Kline Hyatt mused on this. Finally he shrugged.

"Judge Carmody will probably have my star and skin me alive for considering such a thing. But there are times when the simple, direct way is the best way. Maybe this is one of such. Come along!"

15.

ONLY THREE MEN were in the Golden Horn. Duke Royale stood behind the bar, and across from him, toying with a whiskey glass he'd just gulped empty, was Meade Bastian. Like the combine rider who had shown earlier to summon Doc Parris, Bastian wore the seedy, battered look which sleeplessness and danger and the rasp of rough elements could place on a man.

Then there was Ollie Ladd. Too full of plain brute endurance to show the effects of the night as Bastian did, Ollie paced up and down the length of the barroom, prowling like a caged animal, dark with frustration, and charged with the hatreds and anger brewed by it. This same frustration was a smoldering fire in the black eyes of Duke Royale and the pale silver ones of Meade Bastian.

"They wouldn't close in," said Bastian, in the obsessed, droning monotone which repetition could occasion. "I sent them around on both sides and told them to close in. They circled, but that was all; they wouldn't close in. The chance shot which knocked Jacklyn out of the saddle right at the start of things, must have turned their livers white. Only Mitch Starker and Ed Hurst followed orders. They went in from the front. They didn't come out. Because the rest quit like dogs and wouldn't close in—!"

The twin doors of the saloon swung and Sheriff Kline Hyatt stepped through. Gil Yeager was with him. For a moment they stood, their glances raking the room swiftly. Then Hyatt tramped ahead, while Yeager swung over to the end of the bar, hooked his left elbow on the top of this and so stood, gravely waiting and watching.

For a little time there was no reaction. Duke Royale, Meade Bastian and Ollie Ladd were men taken by surprise and struck with momentary indecision. Then Bastian pushed away from the bar and slowly wheeled to fully face Yeager and Hyatt. Duke Royale remained motionless, without expression, his inky eyes unrevealing of thought or emotion.

Ollie Ladd ceased his pacing, but was too full of explosive feeling to remain completely still. He began a weaving motion from side to side, rocking from one foot to the other in a ponderous tramping. Watching, Gil Yeager thought that at this moment Ollie Ladd resembled nothing so much as a cornered bear, reared upright and about to bawl with fury and go into headlong charge. But, knowing that Kline Hyatt's attention would be centered on Ollie, Yeager kept his close watch of Meade Bastian and Duke Royale.

Particularly of Duke Royale. Not only because of a warning Cam Reeves had given, but because of the poised stillness of the man and the utter lack of expression in face or eye which somehow suggested a danger and a deadliness not apparent in Meade Bastian. For in Bastian's look his feelings were plain; all his anger and frustration easily recognized. Bastian could be read, his likely intent reasonably guessed. But there was no reading Duke Royale. Therefore, as Yeager saw it, he was the more dangerous of the two.

Now, through the hiatus of suspended sound, Kline Hyatt's words struck bluntly.

162

"Ollie, I want you!"

Ollie's answer was a heavy growl. "You want me—what for? Don't come with any mealy mouth talk about pinning a deputy's star on me again. I'm not interested. If I ever wear a star again, it'll be the one you pack."

Kline Hyatt stared, then barked a short, mirthless laugh. "Why, Ollie—don't tell me you got ambitions? That you'd be sheriff? It's way too late for that. I'm not here to offer you a star again. I'm here to arrest you."

Now it was Ollie's turn to stare. He even ceased that bear-like, back and forth swaying. His words erupted gutturally from his thick throat.

"Arrest me! What for?"

"For the murder of Cress Lucas!"

The physical stillness in Ollie Ladd grew. "You're crazy," he blurted. "You know as well as I do, who killed Lucas. The man you came in here with, did it. Yeager!"

Kline Hyatt shook his head. "No, Ollie, that old claim won't do—it won't do at all. I've got direct testimony from Brick Rand, as well as the word of an eye witness. You shot Lucas in the back, Ollie—deliberately and, as the law puts it, with malice aforethought. Which makes it cold-blooded murder, Ollie. And I'm arresting you for it. I'll take your gun!"

Ponderous of mind and thought as well as of body, it took Ollie Ladd a little time to accept the full meaning of Kline Hyatt's words and to react to them. When he did, finally, it was with the berserk, animal-like fury which had been seething in him and which now burst blindly forth. He mumbled something which was unintelligible, and when he reached for his gun it was frighteningly apparent it was not for the purpose of surrendering the weapon to Hyatt.

Kline Hyatt's cry was sharp with bitter warning.

"Don't try it, Ollie. You fool—don't try it!"

He might as well have yelled at a great wind, and, realizing it, Hyatt crouched and drew his gun.

The very physical bulk of Ollie Ladd which made the

massive power in him so imposing, also slowed him in movement to some degree. So, even though he started for his weapon ahead of Kline Hyatt, when the room shuddered before the first crashing report, it was Hyatt who had got away the shot.

Ollie grunted under a bullet's impact, which, huge as he was, spun him half around and left him staggering, while the slug he'd intended for Hyatt, fired now purely by muscular reaction, dug a splintering way into the bar front, not a yard to one side of Meade Bastian. And this set Bastian off.

Fully committed to this thing now, Kline Hyatt saw Bastian start into action, so put his second bullet into the center of Bastian's chest. Meade Bastian took a single step forward, coughed and went down on his face.

Ollie Ladd, swinging desperately back for another try at Hyatt, ran into the third slug from the sheriff's gun. Ollie's mouth sagged open and his eyes went blankly staring. He dropped his gun, walked straight into the front of the bar, clung to it a moment with outthrown arms and clawing hands, then slipped away from it and slithered to the floor, giving up a great, tired sigh before going completely still.

The rumble of the guns had been a great tumult of sound in the confines of the barroom. Now this tumult had ceased and a momentary silence came down so complete that even the smallest of sounds thundered in a man's ears.

Such as the thin, tight, indrawing of breath by Duke Royale. He was leaning far out across the bar, staring down at Meade Bastian's huddled figure. And now that indrawing of breath became a breaking cry.

"Meade—Meade—!"

There was more in this cry than just the concern of a friend for a friend. It went deeper than that; there was a blood tie in it. Observing and listening, Gil Yeager knew that Cam Reeves had been guessing right. Here was relationship, as brother for brother.

As that cry rang out, Duke Royale pushed back and

straightened up, and his face, so much an expressionless mask before, now was twisted and wild, and out of those obsidian black eyes blazed the darkest of grief-sharpened hatred. From a shelf beneath the bar, Duke Royale caught up a short-barreled, heavy caliber revolver and pushed the muzzle toward Sheriff Kline Hyatt.

At the moment, Hyatt was motionless, a lank, stooped figure, his glance and full attention on Ollie Ladd, the strong shadow of sadness and regret in his eyes and across his face. And Duke Royale had him dead to rights.

Never afterward was Gil Yeager able to clearly recall the sequence of mental and physical impulse which governed his own movements in the next split second. He knew only that he saw and recognized Duke Royale's intent. Then, somehow, his own gun was clear of the leather, was stabbing level and bucking in recoil.

He saw invisible force strike Royale and drive him to one side, saw a strange, flaccid shrinkage overcome all the force and fire in the man. And then Duke Royale was slipping from sight behind the bar, while the gun he held, still unfired, thumped heavily on the floor.

They were back in Kline Hyatt's office. As thoroughly drained and beaten out physically and emotionally as he had ever been in his life, Gil Yeager slouched deep in a chair. Behind the desk Kline Hyatt sat, hunched of shoulder, dry and still of feature, a man seemingly far removed from the lank, wolf-fast instrument of death he'd been in the Golden Horn but a few hours before. Like Yeager, he also was burdened with a great weariness.

Following the shoot-out in the Golden Horn, a tumult of excitement had held the town. Men had crowded the saloon with their questions and their wonder. Johnny Hock had been there, and Patch Kelly and Bill Spelle and all others close to the scene. Finally there had been Judge Carmody, stern and demanding, and to him Kline Hyatt had given the story, simply, starkly and in blunt detail. And when he had done, Judge Carmody left without charge or recrimination, merely shaking his head in regret over the misguided ways of some men, and of the bitterly final results these ways could bring.

So now it was done, and Gil Yeager sat with his weariness and his thoughts, and it seemed there was no great purpose left in life for him.

Finally stirring, Kline Hyatt scuffed through a drawer in his desk and came up with a star. He tossed this to Yeager.

"That's the one I took off Ollie Ladd. When you head home, swing over by the lake and throw this star out into it. I owe Ollie that much—to see that the badge he wore will never be worn by another man. Which, I suppose, makes you think me a hypocritical damn fool?"

Pocketing the star, Yeager shook his head slowly.

"Not at all. While a man's alive, you see and know the worst in him. Afterwards, well—you remember the times you knew him in the better light."

"That's it," Kline Hyatt said. "There was a lot of brute animal in Ollie Ladd, but I can recall times when a spell of good nature showed in him and then he was like an amiable, harmless bear. At such times I was close to being fond of him." Spurred by these thoughts, Hyatt's voice rang with a quick, harsh bitterness. "This star I wear—the star any lawman wears—sometimes it can become the cruelest damn taskmaster ever designed—!"

Reared upright in his chair, Hyatt now sagged back again, and in dark mood went on.

"Tonight I'm going to buy myself a bottle of whiskey, and before I manage to get to sleep I'll probably be looking at the bottom of it."

Gil Yeager rode home through sundown's rich, softening glow. At the Rubicon Creek crossing he reined over to the lake edge and threw the star Kline Hyatt had given him well out into the depths, where it made a tiny splash and set a few small ripples stirring.

From a nearby tule clump a mallard called. A white crane was an ivory statue at the edge of a shallows, and against the sunset sky a cloud of blackbirds wheeled and swung in last flight before seeking roost against the approach of night.

Out of this vista of earth and sky and water, with its space and its color and its great primary stillness, there came a sudden sense of peace which startled Yeager, and miraculously relaxed him. He sat his saddle motionless for a moment, marveling that this could be; that a man could go through the stress of extreme danger, that he could look upon and deal out violent death, know a degree of grief and regret, and still emerge from it all with balance and a surge of suddenly renewed purpose.

When he rode in at Lazy Y, Cam Reeves was there, waiting in the dusk.

"Was beginning to think you wouldn't show up," Cam said gruffly. "You're to come along to Long B with me."

"No need of that," Yeager said carefully. "I can—"

"Plenty of need," Cam cut in. "After what you been through today is no time for you to be alone. Burke and me, we took care of things around here. Sort of cleaned up for you. So now you come along. Laurie's orders, if you must know."

Laurie! Laurie the lovely, the gentle one—of the gay, head-tossing little laugh—! Abruptly Yeager was eager.

When he and Cam Reeves splashed through the little ditch ford at the end of the lane and started across the interval toward the ranchhouse, it was as if she had heard them. For the door opened and she stood there, slender and lightly poised against the lamp-glow beyond. And when he stepped from his saddle she came to the edge of the porch to meet him.

"Maybe I've no right to face you, Laurie," he said. "For I've been a long way down into the depths. I've wallowed around in a lot of hate and there's the blood of dead men on me."

On tiptoe she stood, reaching to put soft fingertips against his lips.

"Hush!" she said gently. "All that matters is that you are here."

Matt Stuart was the byline used by L.P. Holmes on a number of outstanding Western novels. Born in a snowed-in log cabin in the heart of the Rockies near Breckenridge Colorado in 1895, Holmes moved with his family when very young to northern California and it was here that his father and older brothers built the ranch house where Holmes grew up and where, in later life, he would live again. He published his first story—"The Passing of the Ghost"—in *Action Stories* (9/25). He was paid ½c a word and received a check for $40. "Yeah—forty bucks," he said later. "Don't laugh. In those far-off days . . . a pair of young parents with a three-year-old son could buy a lot of groceries on forty bucks." He went on to contribute nearly 600 stories of varying lengths to the magazine market as well as to write over fifty Western novels under his own name and Matt Stuart. For the many years of his life, Holmes would write in the mornings and spend his afternoons calling on a group of friends in town, among them the blind Western author Charles H. Snow whom Lew Holmes always called "Judge" Snow (because he was Napa's Justice of the Peace 1920–1924) and who frequently makes an appearance in later novels as a local justice in Holmes's imaginary Western communities. Holmes's Golden Age as an author was from 1948 through 1960. During these years under his Matt Stuart byline he produced such notable novels as *Dusty Wagons*, *Gunlaw at Vermillion*, *Wire in the Wind*, *Sunset Rider*, and *Gun Smoke Showdown*. This last was reprinted in paperback under the title *Saddle-man*. In these novels one finds the themes so basic to his Western fiction: the loyalty which unites one man to another, the pride one must take in his work and a job well done, the innate generosity of most of the people who live in Holmes's ambient Western communities, and the vital relationship between a man and a woman in making a better life.